SANCTIONED KILL

(A Kyra Ray Novel)

CR HIATT

NOTE FROM AUTHOR

Sanctioned Kill is the first in the series featuring, Kyra Ray, and was adapted from the screenplay originally titled, Retribution, written in 2009.

The story was first published as part of The Hot Box set, along with 7 other thrillers from best-selling authors in both the United States and the United Kingdom, and was an International Best-Seller, hitting the top 50 in the UK and #1 in 7 different categories.

ACKNOWLEDGEMENT

Thank you to the men and women who either serve in the military, or in a civilian capacity to keep this country safe, and to their allies who fight alongside them.

This book is a work of fiction. Names, characters, places, and incidents are products of the author's imagination or have been used fictitiously and are not to be construed as real. Some liberties were taken when describing actions in certain locales. Any resemblance to persons, living or dead, actual events or locales or organizations is entirely coincidental.

AMB
C & C
Printed in the United States of America

Cover design by David C. Cassidy
http://davidccassidy.com/

INTERNATIONAL BEST-SELLER TOP 50 IN THE UK AS PART OF THE HOT BOX SET

Compelled by her past, Kyra Ray enlisted in the military at the age of 18, giving up an international modeling contract, and was hand-picked to train as an operative for an anti-terror unit (ATU).

Because of his past, Dalton LeClair became a highly-paid assassin.

***

Destined for Danger. Sanctioned to Kill.

Hot on the trail of an international weapons ring, covert agent Kyra Ray finds herself caught in the cross-hairs of a ruthless arms dealer in the perilous mountains of war-torn Afghanistan. Closing in, the mission takes an unexpected and near-deadly turn in the high-stakes drama of New York City, where Kyra is mysteriously spared by an assassin sent to kill. Retrained as an assassin and given strict orders to take him down, Kyra becomes trapped in a game of cat-and-mouse that will put her life on the line and her directive to the test—her sanction to kill.

Kyra Quote: "Are you telling me this assassin became infatuated with me to the point he killed other agents, but felt compelled to save me because of self indulgent lust from afar?"

Table of Contents

"Don't wound a snake; kill it..." ~ Harriet Tubman

CHAPTER 1

Mountains of Virginia

Dressed in jogging gear—sports top, neoprene tights, and a pair of *Nike* running shoes—Kyra Ray sat on a stool in the center of a cellar room with her hands cuffed behind her back, a square bucket of water on a table in front of her, and a lone light bulb dangling overhead.

The floors were mud and dirt, the walls concrete without any windows, and the rancid smell of urine and vomit—from victims there before her—filled her nostrils and made her want to puke, but this was not some hidden cave in the mountains of Afghanistan; this was somewhere in the heart of America.

Two interrogators in dark fatigues and black masks flanked her on both sides bellowing out a barrage of questions. They grilled her in English, Pashto, Urdu, and Arabic dialects, and then followed up with jabs to the gut when she refused to answer.

To amuse herself during the grilling, Kyra made up names for the two men. The one on her left she referred to as Stubby, because he was short and stout. The other one she referred to as, Hulk, because he was huge and lumbered over her 5'10" frame.

They had been at it for a while. Her body was drenched in sweat, her long hair hanging down over her eyes, and red blotches remained on her face, arms, and abs from the pummelling she received.

"Tell me your name!" Stubby bellowed out once again in English then Arabic.

Silence.

Hulk hauled off and backhanded her across the cheek. Her head snapped to the side, but when she turned back around to face him—her tongue tasting blood from the new cut on her lip—she gave him a smart-assed smirk.

"You just got deleted from my Christmas card list."

"Enough with the wisecracks," he bellowed, and responded with a gut punch under the ribs that sucked the air out of her lungs then he followed up with the same round of questions.

"Give us your name!"

Silence.

"Who do you work for?"

Silence.

"What is your mission?"

She stared straight ahead then found a spot on the wall and let her mind focus on it.

Stubby grabbed a hold of her long hair and forced her face down in the bucket of water then held her there for several seconds. Her body shook as she struggled to breathe.

He pulled her head back out, giving her a moment of freedom. "How long you wanna play this game?"

Silence.

Splash, back down into the water, waited a few seconds, and then pulled her free. "You think this'll go easier because you're a woman? Do we look like we give a rat's ass?"

Silence.

He forced her down again, holding her there longer than he did the times before. Her body convulsed, like that of someone having a seizure as she struggled to breathe. When he finally pulled her free, she coughed up water then spit it at him, which pissed him off enough to force her down one more time.

"Pull her up," Hulk ordered after a few seconds. "I know what will make her talk."

Stubby reluctantly pulled her free.

"Big mistake messin' with us sloth!" Hulk said as he put his hooded face up to hers. "We've been doing this a long time. Know everything about you, so give me your name!"

Still defiant, Kyra couldn't help herself. She flipped the wet hair out of her face and glared at the hooded man before her with a gleam in her eyes that was hard to miss. "If you know everything about me, you already know my name, dickhead."

Another smack hit her hard across the face. The force of the blow knocked her off her ass and sent her flying, her feet kicked over the table and bucket of water on the way down. She landed on her shoulder. The pain immediate, forcing her to grit her teeth to keep from screaming, not wanting to give them the satisfaction.

Stubby placed the stool upright then grabbed her and roughly positioned her back on the stool, while Hulk put his hooded face up close to her ear.

"Give us the answers to our questions, or we'll start using that body for something better than a punching bag! I know what happened to you, what makes you go off the rail."

He grabbed a hold of her hair and yanked her head back, hard, straining her neck and letting her know he was in control. Using his other hand, he stroked the side of her face and provocatively moved it down her neck then over the shoulder, continuing down the arm and over her chest in a sexual manner, trying to humiliate her and force her to act.

Her body went stiff and she sent him a scathing look, verifying that this intimidation technique was causing her to react.

"We've had enough dancing around," he said, taunting her as he continued to show his dominance over her. "Now it's time we make use of your assets."

He pulled his hand free from her hair and touched the strap of her sports top, making her think he was going to slide it off her shoulder.

Her eyes bounced back and forth between the two hooded tormentors, only now there was a fire in them that wasn't there a moment ago.

"Don't do it," she said to them through clenched teeth. "You'll regret it."

Stubby and Hulk glanced at each other through the eyes in the mask and chuckled.

"Yeah...?" Stubby said, mocking her. Following Hulk's lead, he trailed his hand over her other shoulder.

She kept her eyes locked on them, not letting them notice the movement behind her back. She snapped the joints in the thumb of her right hand, and then folded it over into the palm making it as flexible as a rubber glove.

"Face it buttercup," Stubby said, mockingly, "we're in control here, not you."

Wrong thing to say!

She tilted her head slightly downward toward her chin, giving off the appearance that she was mortified, which made them smile.

Then simultaneous events occurred before either one of them realized what was happening. She kicked her left foot up and connected with Stubby's groin, causing him to grab his crotch and buckle over, stunned by her strength.

Tilting her head back, slightly, she took aim—using her forehead—then lunged forward toward Hulk's nose making him take a step back.

Her right hand now free of the cuffs, she grabbed the stool underneath her, swung it around and found a mark upside Hulk's head.

14

With his massive size he was only dazed, so she followed it up with a roundhouse kick to the other side of his head. As he stumbled, she cracked the stool over his back knocking him to the ground.

CHAPTER 2

Mike Brady and Barry West, case officers for the Anti-Terror Unit (ATU), stood on the other side of a one-way mirror observing the interrogation.

ATU was a small covert ops organization under the guidance of West, a former CIA operative retired from field duty after suffering a hearing loss from an explosion at the American Embassy while serving in Iraq, but with the express permission of the President. At present, they were handling threat assessment issues involving the Taliban, al Qaeda, and other insurgents in the Afghanistan/Pakistan region, though clandestine operations for this small team of operators had no borders. Funded by private investors, ATU was not officially recognized or affiliated with the CIA, affording them the capacity to investigate hostile situations around the world, as well as giving them the mobility to move around the US when the need arose.

The offices were located in a non-descript warehouse building away from the day-to-day bureaucracy of official intelligence agencies, but even though they were off the books, a team of officers with the National Clandestine Services was tasked with overseeing things behind the scenes in D.C.

West took a swig of the turbo-charged coffee he purchased on the way to the office earlier that morning and glanced over at Brady with a knowing look. "What'd I tell you?"

"This is the third POW training she's gone through in the last six months," Brady said, mildly irritated. "Why do you keep putting her through it?"

"I'm not puttin' her through shit; she keeps requesting it."

"Why? To what end?"

West shrugged. "Said she wants to keep reminding herself of what it was like being held captive."

Brady grunted. "You think that's healthy? Hardly the same; we're not the enemy, so the mindset wouldn't be there. This is child's play compared to what she went through in the hands of insurgents. It's almost like she's punishing herself."

"Who am I to question her mindset," West said, off-handedly, not understanding the issue he was raising. "Maybe she just needs to be pushed until she feels like she's not in control. Anything that helps her prepare for the field. Hell, you and I went through the same training; we had it just as bad."

Brady shook his head. He didn't agree the fact that West signed off on the continuous training, but now was not the time to argue the point. He had a reconnaissance op to prepare for, and knew if he pissed off West he could turn around and quash the mission. "How'd she get out of those cuffs?"

"One of the injuries she sustained from her confinement, apparently. It's in her file," West chided, reminding Brady he should have read it. "They broke the joints in her right hand. Now, she can slip the thumb out at will, plus the fact that she is double-jointed."

Brady studied her. "Which proves my point, she could have gotten out of those cuffs at any time. She wanted them to smack her around and push her into acting."

"Like I said; whatever works..."

***

Mike Brady was a member of Special Ops before being asked to join the Anti-Terror Unit. He had been to hell and back more times than he could remember, worked with hundreds of men and women in uniform and civilian alike, tough individuals, but the woman on the other side of the mirror was an enigma. That was one of the reasons he originally requested her for his team, and the fact that she was young enough that he could play a part in her operative training.

She inherited her Armenian Mother's dark hair and skin, and spoke various languages, so could easily blend in, provided she wore contacts to hide the blue eyes from her father's side of the family. She was as tough as she was beautiful, and from what he had observed, was constantly pushing herself to surpass the high expectations she placed on herself, even those of some of her peers. Brady just hoped she could harness that anger she wore like a shield of armor, and use it to their advantage when they were out in the field.

He knew why she wore that wall of protection. Hell, he didn't blame her. If anyone had the right to be angry, Kyra Ray did.

Like so many others, life as she knew it changed on September 11, 2001 when she lost both parents. They were passengers on American Airlines Flight 77, one of the planes hijacked by terrorists and then flown into the Pentagon killing everyone on board, and taking the lives of one-hundred-twenty-five victims inside the building.

The loss was the climactic event that convinced her to join the military on the day of her eighteenth birthday, giving up a million-dollar modeling contract offered by an International magazine.

With those feelings guiding her she excelled in the military; served three tours in Afghanistan, and took part in the Female Engagement Team (FET)—a program that reached out to the Afghani women and children. She learned the local languages, won some awards, and made friends along the way, turning them into informants later.

Then her world was shattered once again. While helping Afghani families near the Afghanistan and Pakistan border, a group of insurgents ambushed the small team of Special Forces she was traveling with, killing some of them and taking others hostage. Those in the hands of the enemy suffered through weeks of humiliating torture before a second team of Spec Ops learned the location of where they were being held and launched a raid on the compound.

***

Brady and West turned their attention back to the mirror. Kyra had Hulk in a headlock on the floor, threatening to squeeze if Stubby came close.

West rapped on the one-way mirror, and spoke into a microphone on the wall. "Give it a rest, Kyra! It's just a POW drill *which you requested.*"

Kyra glared toward the wall where the voice came from. "Yeah, well this POW escaped."

"Great," West said sarcastically. "So you're a hero."

Brady flinched and darted an angry look toward West, as he placed his hand over the microphone. "Don't be an ass, she doesn't deserve that."

West shrugged indifferently, as he took another sip of his coffee. "Just trying to speed things along, we've all got work to do."

Brady removed his hand from the mic. "Kyra, I've got something that needs our attention. Could you hit the showers then join us over in Ops."

Kyra reluctantly let go of Hulk, snapped her thumb back into place and grabbed a couple of towels off a rack. "Thanks for the session boys," she mocked as she headed toward the exit door.

CHAPTER 3

Dubai, United Arab Emirates

Dalton LeClair entered the Pub in the lobby of the Marina Byblos Hotel, just to the rear of the Dubai Marina Yacht Club where he docked his Silverton Motor Yacht just two days prior.

Before removing his aviator sunglasses he did a quick sweep of the room, checking for anyone who looked like they didn't belong, or could possibly pose a threat. A man in his line of work—whether by choice, or not—always had to watch his back.

There were only two empty stools at the horseshoe-shaped bar; the others occupied by men whom he assumed were expats enjoying a pint of beer after a day of doing business in Dubai.

There were strict rules on drinking and gambling in the United Arab Emirates, but a license or permit could be acquired to drink in certain locations; the pubs and bars in hotels being on the list.

Several men, with journalist I.D. badges clipped to their shirts, were scattered around the billiards tables with their eyes glued to the tennis match playing out on a Sport's Channel on a big-screen Plasma TV.

In the center of the joint, two tables had been pushed together to accommodate seven young women,

21

who appeared to be flight attendants, sipping colorful drinks and admiring the selection of men.

At another occupied table, a man and woman had their chairs pushed together like that of a couple on a romantic date, only this duo seemed to be engaged in an argument while the plate of appetizers in front of them were probably getting cold. The raised voices from their heated debate verified to Dalton that the only threat they posed was to each other.

Once he deemed the Pub secure, he removed his sunglasses and slipped them into the inside pocket of his leather bomber jacket then walked to the opposite end of the bar. Grabbing one of the empty stools, he positioned himself with his back to the wall, so he could observe who came and went. When the bartender approached, he ordered a pint of Guinness Blonde— the new American lager he recently sampled which quickly became a favorite, so he was pleased to learn it was distributed in the UAE since there were so many expats living in the area, and tourism was thriving.

While waiting, he continued to observe his surroundings, and noticed one of the young women from the table of seven as she approached the bar. She leaned down on the lacquered finish, and let her eyes dance over each man, looking for someone to buy her a drink, he surmised. After going down the line, she eventually settled on him. Their eyes met, causing her to get lost in the intensity as she studied him.

Intrigued, she offered him a seductive smile. He was used to that. A scar on his left cheek, which had faded over time, did not mar his dark and brooding good looks. Quite the opposite in fact; adding an air of ruggedness to his masculine and tanned face, having him often referred to as the handsome rogue that women seemed to be attracted to.

If he wasn't crunched for time, he might have considered buying her a drink and participating in an hour of mindless chit chat, or anything else she offered. As it was, he was not happy about being summoned.

He cocked his head to the side and shrugged, as if to say; "sorry honey, a hookup's not going to happen tonight". Her lips curved into a pout, until one of the journalists, a *Chris Evans* look-alike, walked up next to her and offered what he couldn't give.

Moments later, the bartender set the mug of amber liquid down in front of him, and he lost interest in the duo as he tried to appear like that of a tourist on vacation. He periodically glanced toward the TVs to check out the sports, and enjoyed the cold liquid quenching his thirst.

A quick glance at his watch revealed forty-five minutes went by without any new visitors, so he took another look around to confirm the dead drop location was secure; no periodic glances his way.

He tossed back the rest of his beer, dropped a pile of cash down on the bar, then slipped off the stool and made his way toward the men's room.

Upon entering, he walked over to the sink and washed his hands, giving him a moment to verify each of the stalls were empty. Both the faucet and air-blower were automatic, so no need to worry about prints. When he was sure he was alone, he walked over to the last stall, entered and locked the door behind him.

Within the confined space, he donned a pair of disposable latex gloves from inside his jacket then removed the tank lid from the toilet to find a waterproof pouch taped on the inside. He retrieved it then put the lid back in place. "*Damn cold war antics*," he thought to himself. He wiped the moisture from the pouch then opened it to retrieve a pre-paid cellphone. When turning it on a text message icon popped up: "Two more players expected @ horse race. Same $$$ entry @ 0700."

He frowned then quickly typed a return message. "Affirmative. See you there."

Powering off the phone, he slipped it into his pocket then dropped the pouch down into the toilet and flushed. After removing the latex gloves, he followed the same procedure, making sure there was no evidence remaining in the bowl before he left the stall. He wiped down any possible fingerprints along the way.

When he passed by the bathroom mirror, he couldn't help but notice the look of resignation in his eyes knowing what the text message meant; that his services were being summoned and saying no was not an option.

Cutting back through the Pub on his way toward the exit, he let his mind wander as he glanced around at the patrons who seemed to be enjoying themselves without any time constraints. He looked forward to the day when he would be able to free himself from the clutches of the group who periodically summoned him to take care of their dirty deeds.

CHAPTER 4

Kyra exited through a steel door and continued down a sterile corridor with industrial tile floor and white walls void of any pictures. Fresh from the shower, she wore faded jeans and a navy-blue army sweatshirt with combat boots on her feet. Even in the casual attire, she could still pass for an international model with her tall, slender build. Long, dark hair fell down over her shoulders, front and back, and the Azure blue eyes, accentuated by thick eyebrows, stood out even more on her sun-kissed skin.

She stopped at a row of vending machines along the way to get a bottle of water and then realized she had no change, everything was at her desk. "Dammit," she muttered to herself. She needed an aspirin.

Even when done correctly a head-butt still gave her a headache. She normally used the self-defense technique as a last resort, but Stubby and Hulk were starting to annoy her, big time. She had to act—even if they were only participating on her request for POW training. She considered apologizing, but then decided against it. They knew the score when they chose to use that technique to push her into action.

Barry West arrived next to her just then. "Here, let me get that," he said as he slipped a dollar bill into the machine. "Least I can do for one of America's heroes."

She glanced toward him and studied his face, unsure of whether or not he was mocking her. "Thanks," she said. Hoping it was just her imagination, she tapped the button for a bottle of water. When it dropped into the bottom drawer, she bent down to retrieve it, opening the cap and gulping down half the bottle.

"You better get to it," West said as he motioned toward a door at the end of the corridor. "Brady is waiting with Tin and J.D."

"Thanks, again," Kyra said, as she headed toward a second steel door with ATU Operation Center on the door. She placed her hand on the biometric lock device just to the right of the door. A green light appeared and the door slid open.

The device had a fingerprint sensor to map the index finger of the individuals on the unit. If anyone else attempted to enter the room, a loud alarm would vibrate through the walls of the building, and an "unauthorized entry" message would alert security personnel, and then transmit data to Langley.

She entered the room. Computers with flat-screen monitors lined the walls. Individual desks with personal laptops, printers, phones, and other necessary equipment for each member of the unit, sat in a semicircle arrangement in the center of the room. That way they could easily communicate with each other when information and alerts came in on the big-screen monitors on the walls ahead of them, displaying satellite images and round-the-clock news coverage. There was also an area set up where Tin—a geek who loved to fiddle around with electrical devices—worked on designing gadgets to be used out in the field.

Brady sat down at the desk in front of the group, and put his feet up. Tin and J.D. were already at work in theirs.

"How was your training this morning, Kyra?"

"Fine," she said with a shrug. "Necessary, though."

"As long as you feel it's helpful," he said, keeping his real thoughts to himself.

She veered over toward her desk, pumping fists with Tin and J.D. along the way. Once she sat down, she popped a couple of aspirin from the top drawer of her desk then grabbed a government issued cell phone and her personal *Samsung Notebook* from the small safe underneath. Her Sig Sauer P226 remained inside.

"Now that the gang's all here, let's get started," Brady said. "Kyra, how do you feel about returning to Afghanistan?"

She instinctively glanced toward the Satellite images that J.D. was reviewing, then turned toward Brady, but tried to keep her expression neutral. Some of the insurgents who held her captive in the mountains of Afghanistan were still free. When the second team of Spec Ops raided the prison compound, there were only a few insurgents on the premises guarding the prisoners; the others were out procuring new weapons.

"What's the op?"

"At this stage it's a simple case of recon and gathering of Intel, nothing more." He glanced over at Tin to elaborate.

"Okay, so check this out," Tin said as his fingers flew over the keys of his computer.

Before joining Agent Brady's team at ATU, Tin worked as a young analyst for military intelligence while serving in the army in Afghanistan, which was where he first met Kyra.

Kyra chuckled when she noticed several empty store-bought cans of *Starbucks Double-Shot Espresso* collecting dust on the floor at Tin's feet. "You know, Tin, you'd probably save some money if you just invested in your own espresso machine."

Tin nodded. "True dat, but then I'd have to learn how to work the machine. Decide which brand of bean to buy then learn how to measure out the right amount of beans with the right amount of water, which would probably take several attempts before I got it just right. Then--"

"Okay, I get it," she said, regretting she opened her big mouth. "I was just sayin'."

J.D. Carroll rolled his eyes. "You know how he likes to go on and on; our little chatty Tin."

J.D. was at his desk reviewing Satellite images coming in from Afghanistan. Earning the cliché nickname, 'Pretty boy', he was a former Air Force Pilot who served two tours in Iraq. He also held a bachelor's degree in political science, a Masters in international affairs, and was fluent in several languages, though his years of studies did not tame his wild and immature ways. If the *Lt. Pete 'Maverick' Mitchell* character in the movie *Top Gun* was six feet tall and had light brown hair with streaked-blond highlights, they would be identical in personality, looks, and attitude.

Kyra smiled. "I'd be chatty too if I ingested that much caffeine during a twenty-four-hour period."

"Don't knock the caffeine," Brady said as he retrieved a tin can of *Revved UP Energy Smokeless Tobacco* from his pocket. Putting the can between his thumb and forefinger, he banged the can a few times, packing the chew. Opened it and grabbed a pinch with his fingers, then stuffed it between his lips and gums.

"That shit's the bomb," J.D. said. He tossed a paper cup to Brady for spit then snatched a can of his own from a small refrigerator under his desk. "You should try it Kyra, helps to keep you awake during those long recon missions."

"Yeah, I think I'll pass," she said. "Getting cancer in the mouth is not my idea of going out in a blaze of glory."

J.D. gazed up at nothing, as if he was in a fantasy, and smiled. "Ah, there's nothing more attractive than a chick with a wad of chew in her mouth."

"Thanks for that," Kyra said, groaning at the blatant image he was conjuring up."

"Could we get back to the matter at hand?" Brady interrupted, internally recalling that his team was still young and sometimes he had to remind them to stay on point. "Tin, you were saying?"

"Right, right ... so you've heard the Intel about the uprising in attacks on military and westerners by the Taliban and insurgents in Afghanistan; Serena Hotel, the Restaurant, among others?"

All business now, each one of them nodded.

"Okay, so we got a communication from one of Brady's assets in the area suggesting he was contacted to broker a weapons deal between, what he believes to be, two major players. I had set up separate email accounts for the asset to contact us then provided him with code words to alert us to the level of significance. He considers the two players to be MVT—Medium Value Targets."

"In other words," Brady added for Kyra's benefit, "they need closer scrutiny because we don't have enough information about them at this time."

"A meet and greet has been scheduled for partial delivery of the product," Tin went on to say. "I'm assuming that's small stuff; guns and ammunition, items that can be easily transported, providing they could pass the security checkpoints. Encrypted messages were attached to the email, so I'm still working on those, but I did find out the identity of one player, or at least the company supplying the weapons: I.G.R."

J.D. snorted. "That's International Gun Runner; just in case you didn't know the entrepreneur spirit has no borders," he joked.

Tin laughed, but nodded in the affirmative. "I.G.R. is a well-known company supplying weapons, ammo, vehicles, choppers, or pretty much anything they can get their hands on to countries and government agencies. Early on they built their reputation by bidding at online auctions then winning the contract out from under some of the major companies; Lockheed, Rayon, etc. Most of their deals seemed to be by the book and legal, on the surface, until I dug a little deeper, and came across some questionable ones. When I scrutinized the paperwork, another name revealed itself, guy by the name of Cash, which is one of many aliases."

Brady put the paper cup up to his mouth and spit. "People only use an alias when they've got something to hide, and they're trying to conceal their true identity," he said for Kyra's benefit. As a young team, it was his job to explain the details of the ops, no matter how miniscule, or obvious in this case, that information might be.

"True dat," Tin said, using one of his favorite phrases.

Kyra glanced at him. "Is the guy for real with these names? International Gun Runner ... Cash?"

Tin gave her one of his confident smiles. "When I discover his real identity, I'm sure he'll be some arrogant guy who thinks he's smarter than everyone else, and tosses out a lot of dough to keep a wall of protection around him."

"Either that, or a secretive corporation using him as a front," J.D. mused. He may be the more immature member of the group, having the propensity to behave like a teenager at times, but he also held a cynical view when it came to what he perceived to be the criminal element.

"Bottom line," Brady said, knowing time was critical, "Tin and I think these guys are providing weapons; and possibly even further training to Taliban and insurgent forces. Assaults have kicked up all across Afghanistan. We already know they were trying to interfere with the voting process. Now, with the recent attacks on locations where westerners and expats hangout, we think they might be trying to play a role in the decision process for the removal of troops. Even if there is a major pull out, we all know there will still be troops in country, which means they'll be in harm's way."

"So what's your plan?" Kyra said, wanting to do all she could to help the troops. She used to be one of them.

"We'll fly in on a cargo jet carrying supplies," Brady continued "do a little surveillance, snap some photos, and get any Intel we can on the players. If we come across anything urgent, we'll call in a team of Spec Ops, and then we're out of there." He paused for a moment. "But before you say you're all in, you need to remember any mission we engage in will be off the books, even as far as ATU is concerned."

Kyra frowned. "Meaning?"

"From the mouth of Barry West; he will not ask the higher ups behind this organization to sign off on a mission—or in his words a fishing expedition—when there is still no signed agreement between the two countries allowing troops to remain."

"So if this simple case of recon turns belly up, you're on your own, literally," J.D. said.

Kyra shook her head, mildly frustrated. "I thought that was the whole purpose of this black ops unit; to handle situations that couldn't go through official channels? Oh, I get it; you mean ATU won't even bail us out if we run into trouble."

"West says this is how it's gotta be; at least right now, for this situation," Brady said, shrugging. "I'm guessing nobody wants any fallout from President Karzai. Mine is not to question why."

"So when do we leave?" she finally said, knowing she would never turn down an opportunity to help the troops.

"Soon as you and I complete our obligatory meeting with the doc," Brady said.

Kyra groaned.

"J.D., secure a safe house with the necessary items we might need while in country, and the transportation to get us there from the base."

"Roger that."

"Tin, we need papers to get us in and out of the country then keep working on those encrypted messages and the real identity of the individual behind I.G.R. Oh, and get photographs of the asset and his bodyguard to Kyra, so she can study them beforehand."

"You got it."

Kyra raised her eyebrows, curious. "The asset has a bodyguard?"

"These days, everybody has a bodyguard in Afghanistan," Brady said. "Working security in war torn countries pays big money...long as you can stay alive to spend it."

Sarcastic laughter filled the room.

Kyra got up out of her seat, wishing her next task could be as uncomplicated as theirs. "Great, I guess I'm off to get analysed; that's worse than getting a root canal without the laughing gas or novocaine."

CHAPTER 5

Langley, Virginia

Seated behind a cherry wood desk, Dr. Nancy Thompson tapped her pencil on a notepad, and patiently observed Kyra sitting on the edge of a leather chair looking as if she was scheming for ways to make a fast escape. Dr. Thompson was a psychologist hired to help the operatives cope with their experiences and prepare them for missions.

Kyra couldn't help but think she looked more like her physical education teacher back in high school, with her dark-blue running suit, brown hair pulled back in a tight pony-tail revealing the gray roots growing in, and the prescription glasses with tinted lenses that dangled on a chain around her neck.

"So you're telling me that delving into my thoughts will help to determine if I am fit to go out in the field?"

"Not necessarily."

"Then what the hell am I doing here?"

Dr. Thompson ignored her remark. "But, it does help to gauge how you might react to certain situations when out in the field."

Appearing bored with the whole process Kyra twirled a strand of hair in her fingers in an effort to hide the real thoughts going on inside of her.

Dr. Thompson glanced down at the report on her desk. "You joined the military on the day of your eighteenth birthday, knowing you could be shipped off to Iraq or Afghanistan immediately after boot camp. What was on your mind when you did that?"

"Is that a serious question?" Kyra asked, and then continued when all she got was a pair of stubborn eyes staring back at her. "I wanted to serve my country, like the thousands of others who volunteer every day."

"You served two tours in Afghanistan then volunteered for a third, even after losing many of your fellow soldiers and friends. A member of your unit said you seemed to have a death wish, continuously putting yourself in harm's way. What do you think of his assessment?"

Kyra shook her head, mildly amused. "No disrespect Doc but you're taking his comment too literally. Miles Davis, my so-called friend and fellow soldier, was being sarcastic suggesting I might be happier at home, married with the white picket fence and a couple of kids running around. He would never have made those comments if I was man, or didn't look the way I do."

Dr. Thompson raised her eyebrows at the frank response. "You are a striking woman. I can't help but wonder if those attributes were a deterrent in the field, or possibly used against you?"

Kyra let out a heavy sigh. She knew what the doc was getting at, but wasn't saying it outright. She wanted to know if Kyra ever dealt with sexual harassment from her fellow brothers in arms, but more importantly, she wanted to know if Kyra was raped during her time in captivity. It was the question on everyone's mind, but one Kyra refused to discuss, except with the officials who demanded the truth. She didn't think her looks were a matter for discussion. Was the torture of rape any worse than the physical torture the men suffered through?

"We all bleed red when wearing military BDU's and standing on the front lines, Doc, looks don't enter the equation there, and they shouldn't be significant here."

Dr. Thompson studied her for a moment, and then let the matter drop. "Fair enough; then let's switch gears. I'd like to talk about your parents."

Kyra shifted in her seat. "My parents?"

Dr. Thompson gave Kyra a penetrating stare. "It would help to know how their death has affected you, and how it plays a role in the choices you make."

Kyra slowly stood up and started to pace the room, fidgeting with objects and obviously uncomfortable. "A day doesn't go by that I don't see the image of the plane going into the building."

"And what goes through your mind when that happens?"

Kyra stopped pacing and sent a glaring look toward Dr. Thompson. "What goes through my mind? Why don't you just come out and ask me what it is you want to know?"

"What is it you think I want to know?"

"That's good; answer the question with a question. You want to know the same thing I ask myself every day; you want to know if I joined the military to get revenge for my parents."

"Did you?"

"Well if I did," she said in a voice riddled with sarcasm, "I suck at it, considering I have zero kills behind me, and was viewed as more of a PR vehicle for the Female Engagement Team. So how's that for your revenge theory, doc?"

Dr. Thompson didn't waiver. "What about now?"

"What about now?"

"Did you sign on to become a covert operative so that you could enact revenge on the enemy?"

"They came looking for me, doc, not the other way around."

A knock on the door gave her a moment to decide how to continue when Brady opened the door and stuck his head in. "Sorry doc, I need to confiscate Kyra." Turning toward her, he said, "They're waiting for us."

Dr. Thompson raised her eyebrows. "Agent Brady, I haven't completed my assessment."

Agent Brady nodded. "Duly noted, doc, but it's just a simple case of recon. As her handler I'll take full responsibility."

Suddenly eager to get out of there, Kyra shot toward the door. "Sorry doc, I know you wanted to bait me, but..."

Dr. Thompson shook her head, frustrated that she couldn't get the response she was looking for. "We will finish this, Kyra!"

"Thanks for the save," Kyra said as they marched down the hall.

Brady gave her an appraising stare. "You know, the doc is not the enemy. Might do you good if you talk about things, what happened to your parents, you..."

Kyra's forehead creased with worry lines. "Was it easy for you to open up and share when you returned; you served in both Iraq and Afghanistan?"

He smiled, knowing she was turning the tables on him. "Sorry hotshot, we're not talking about me."

She nodded. "I'll get there, I just need more time."

He kept his eyes on her for a moment, and then nodded. "Okay then, grab your gear and make sure you have your bullet-proof vest—level IV armor with plate inserts. The Stan is still a volatile war zone; wheels up in thirty."

CHAPTER 6

Kabul, Afghanistan

Wearing a dark-colored *hijab* and brown contacts to hide her vibrant blue eyes, Kyra walked among a group of Afghani men in traditional dress and women in Burqas on a dust-filled street in Kabul, Afghanistan trying to blend in while others peddled their goods at the local markets nearby.

Her eyes periodically darted toward the front of a seedy hotel; a rat trap of a place if ever there was one, compared to the five-star Serena Hotel where westerners were targets of Taliban insurgents not too long ago.

She instantly became alert when a man resembling the picture she studied back at ops, exited the hotel carrying a stainless steel briefcase. According to Brady, the man referred to himself by the name, Thomas Hadley, when in reality, he was a former insurgent who tired of hiding out in the caves of Pakistan when he got a taste of the lifestyle money could provide during a few trips to Dubai—known as the Las Vegas of the Middle East.

He was wiry thin with thick, dark hair and bushy eyebrows, but instead of wearing the loose fitting pants and shirt like most of the local men, he wore a pair of linen pants, a polo shirt with a scarf around his neck, and leather sandals on his feet.

The man following him like a cheap suit was Lars Fuchs, his bald, tattoo-covered bodyguard, even though he kept those attributes hidden with a New York Yankees baseball cap and a long-sleeved khaki shirt so he didn't draw attention to the two of them.

Fuchs originally came to Afghanistan as a private security contractor for a real estate developer helping with the rebuilding efforts from the war, then went freelance when he was offered a steady supply of tax-free dough deposited into an off shore account, and with no questions asked.

"Tracking device in place," Brady's voice echoed through the eraser-size earpiece in her ear once the subjects were on their way up the street.

"I love it," Kyra said into the mic, her tone filled with mockery. "We're tracking our own asset."

"Just get your eyes on the subject, hotshot."

Dressed in a brown Shalwar kameez with a scarf wrapped around his head, Kyra had a little trouble picking Brady out among the locals until she noticed his distinctive swagger as he slipped out the door of the hotel, and gave her a perfunctory nod before he ambled off in the opposite direction.

He claimed to have picked up his unique walk after receiving too many hits to the groin during his college years on the Rugby field. When he became an operative he considered changing his gait, but his wife—a fashion designer until she gave birth to twin girls—said it was one of the traits she was attracted to when they met, so the swagger remained.

"Affirmative," Kyra said. Acknowledging the signal, she picked up the tail and followed the pair from a discreet distance as they walked along the shops on Chicken Street.

The two men passed a butcher chopping goods on an outdoor table. Unlike the markets she was used to, the carcasses dangled from hooks right along the street, and donkeys—carting baskets of goods on their bare backs—moseyed alongside them while Afghani women weaved carpets for all to see.

They stopped in front of an Internet Café with a herd of goats tethered out front, and disappeared inside. Kyra lingered at the outdoor market to admire the hand-woven rugs and traditional scarves known as *Keffiyeh's*, while periodically glancing through the door of the Café.

Inside, local men and teenage boys occupied terminals that lined the walls; some of them enjoying games on the net, while others used the computers to keep in touch with family from faraway.

Keeping their eyes to the ground—as if trying to avoid any kind of security camera—Hadley paid the clerk then the two of them stood in line and waited with others. When it was their turn, they headed toward the back where there was an unoccupied terminal then Hadley sat down and began to type, while Fuchs stood behind him to watch his back.

"So this guy, Hadley, he's the asset, right?" Kyra whispered into the mic.

"Asset, informant, spy, pain in the ass," Brady said through the earpiece. "I call him many names. He's been helpful in the past; giving me the location of planned attacks by the Taliban, and offered up the names of individuals alleged to be involved with al Qaeda. But his main goal is to make money to pay for his insatiable habits and keep him out of living like a pauper, gambling on Thoroughbreds being tops on the list, and women a close second."

"Then why didn't he just stay in Dubai? With those habits he's a little far from the action."

"This is where his connections are; the ones that butter his bread to feed his addictions, and offer him the luxury of traveling. But don't worry, hotshot; now that you've joined my team, you can consider him *our* pain in the ass."

Kyra was touched by the fact that Brady called her 'hotshot'; that was the nickname given to her father during his time in the Marines.

"Okay then, so why are we traipsing around like a couple of shadows on the streets of Kabul, stalking *our* asset, and placing a tracking device on him. Why don't we just go up to him and ask whatever it is we need to know?"

Brady grunted. "Oh ye have so much to learn; like I said, he has many names. Assets are not always on the up and up. You don't always know whose side they're on. Sometimes, they play both. They tend to look out for themselves, and not necessarily the handler whose country is paying for their avid lifestyle. Needless to say, their information can be suspect."

"So he may have coughed up the goods in the past, but we still can't trust him?"

"You've heard the phrase; trust, but verify."

She snorted. "I've also heard the phrase; trust no one."

"Welcome to the world of covert ops."

"That just gives me a warm and fuzzy feeling knowing who we get in bed with," she said, sarcastically. She was only a junior operator, so she knew she had a lot to learn, but it was hard to understand the concept of paying someone to be an informant or asset if you couldn't trust them.

"Nature of the business, I guess," she mumbled to herself seconds later.

Brady refrained from commenting. After all, he had been on the receiving end of a few double-crosses during his career. "Just maintain the motto; trust, but verify."

"I think I'll stick with the one that will help to keep me alive: Trust No One."

Out of the corner of her eye, she noticed a group of locals dressed in traditional garb riding old ten-speed bicycles, weaving in and out of the traffic of used Toyota Trucks and Corollas, common vehicles used by the Afghani people. As they moved past her, she spotted Brady among them; the red hair of his Irish heritage peeking out from underneath the Afghan scarf was a dead giveaway.

He rolled on past the internet Café, then stopped and parked his bike in front of a merchant selling cell phones and accessories, while he pretended to check his own phone to cover the fact that he was observing the two subjects the entire time.

Moments later, Hadley and Fuchs exited the Café with their heads locked together in conversation, and headed back in the direction of the hotel.

"Watch my six," Brady said. When the two of them were out of sight, he slipped in through the door of the café. Moments later, he walked back out flashing a set of pearly whites.

"Hope your stint with the FET got you used to scorpions and camel spiders. We might be lying among them for a few days."

CHAPTER 7

Since the start of the war against the Taliban and insurgents in Afghanistan, millions of dollars from foreign aid, as well as funds from companies and private individuals, passed through the area in the hopes of rebuilding and gearing the country toward democracy. Luxury hotels, condominiums, and even shopping centers—like those seen in places like the United States—took shape in Kabul, Afghanistan. The rebuilding efforts boomed in the capital city. Yet, the majority of the Afghani people still lived in poverty-like conditions.

Unpaved roads, downed streetlights, and crater-size potholes made driving seem like moving through a fast-flowing river with vehicles often driving into oncoming traffic at the roundabouts. Adding to the wars of years past, some bombed out neighborhoods remained, and the destitute children still played in the rubble.

It was ironic that from atop a mound of garbage in the hills, where children combed through the trash looking for metal and things of value to cash in for food, one could look down and view the district of Sherpur, a development unlike any other in Afghanistan, a neighborhood where money flourished, and corruption permeated.

Behind the concrete walls of the newly developed neighborhood, the drug traffickers, warlords, politicians, bankers, and businessmen—getting rich off the streams of money flowing in, bribes, corruption, and the never-ending drug trade—lived in marbled villas and mansions referred to as The Poppy Palaces.

The possible withdrawal of U.S. troops in 2014, and then payoffs to politicians, security forces and police, Taliban and insurgents; the corruption and criminal activity carried out by the wealthy residents in the area, continued and grew without interruption.

Some former residents of Sherpur—too poor to find other accommodations after they were evicted and their homes demolished—pitched tents in the hills above the colorful mansions, and lived like nomads off the land.

While serving on the FET during her second tour in Afghanistan, Kyra and her teammates visited locals hoping to determine the needs of the women and children. It was during one of those trips that she met an Afghani family, Dawood, Hadiah, and their ten-year-old daughter, Sadia, who were living in the Sherpur District, before the redevelopment efforts. Kyra struck up an unusual friendship with the family, after learning Sadia had a desire to learn American softball, a sport Kyra excelled in during high school.

During a visit to the area, Kyra tossed a rubber ball around with a group of girls while the boys kicked around soccer balls—provided by the troops—and was stunned when she realized Sadia had a natural talent, and even picked up the windmill pitch after a quick lesson. Seeing the girls' enthusiasm, she arranged to have a care package sent from the states, and asked for rubber-coated softballs, gloves, and accessories for the sport, instead of the protein bars, books, magazines, and DVDs that she usually received.

When the team arrived in Kabul, Kyra reached out to that same family, who were more than happy to see her. They were now living with other family members in a village of tents on the hills above Sherpur.

That is why Kyra and Brady were now dressed in desert fatigues, tan scarfs wrapped around their faces, and barely visible lying with their bellies buried in the sand. Using the small village of tents as their cover, they settled in for long, tedious hours of surveillance.

Trying to block out the smells of garbage, sewage, and left-over remnants of whatever had been cooked on the fires, their eyes combed the area using high-end binoculars, switching to night vision when the sun went down. The contours of the hills, boulders left over from the construction efforts, and thick bushes kept them hidden from civilization down below.

They had been at it for close to forty-eight hours, alternating every few to give the other a break or chance for a little shuteye. Brady had just dozed off, but she knew he wouldn't be down for long; he was too wired on caffeine from the thermos of coffee and the wads of Energy Dip he kept stuffing behind his lip.

It was nearing 0430 hours in the morning. The sun was just starting to rise behind the mountains in the distance. Kyra saw very little activity going on at the early morning hour, at least the kind that warranted their attention.

The locals and expats in the Capital City of Kabul were tucked away in the comfort and safety of their respective places of residence, which meant less traffic on the streets, and made it easier to keep an eye on the evil doers.

During the night there was the occasional chase by Afghani police, movement of military apparatus, gunfire and explosions from excursions with small groups of Taliban forces—expected in a war zone. A delivery truck sped down the road causing a raucous, until it was forcibly stopped at a security checkpoint; they had relaxed when the driver and passengers stepped out of the vehicle, revealing it was just a couple of young Afghani men making a delivery.

At 0300 a fire broke out near the airport and had them glued to their lenses, until it was handled by the local fire department. Interesting to watch, but not what they came there to do. On reflection, Kyra couldn't help but think that life in Kabul wasn't much different than some of the major cities in the U.S.A., what with gangs and criminals wreaking havoc on local residents and businesses.

Brady stirred awake beside her a few moments later, stretching and wiping sand from his eyes. "See anything new and exciting during my little cat nap?"

Kyra smiled, and teased, "Yeah, sorry dude, you missed it. The *Victoria Secret* models were here doing a photo shoot for their desert camo bikini line."

Brady groaned, and then rifled through his gear for his can of chew—the breakfast of champions. He opened the tin, pinched three fingers full, and stuffed it inside his lip.

"Just think; *Adriana Lima* and *Alessandra Ambrosio* up close and personal."

"Damn, girl," he said. He dropped the tin back into the pocket of his backpack then snatched the binoculars and proceeded to do a 360 degree sweep of the area. "You couldn't have filled my head with that image before I put my head in the sand?"

"I'm just a lowly junior operative; not in my job description to supply you with the material for your fantasies."

They stopped the small talk for a few moments while both of them methodically checked over the area. They didn't know if the 'players' expected at the meet were already in country, or coming in on a flight from destinations unknown.

"We know the meet is in the Sherpur District," Brady said, motioning the area down below the hill. "I'll do a sweep to the north and south of us, starting on

Airport Road leading from the airport, you check east to west."

"Copy," Kyra said, and she proceeded to do a sweep over Qall E Fatullah, Kuloloa Pushta and moving over into the Shar-E-Now District, just west of Sherpur. She checked all the streets near the Serena Hotel.

"So how'd you wind up meeting a family of nomads?" Brady asked with interest while his binoculars did a sweep over Wazir Akbar Khan.

"They were living in a mud, brick home in Sherpur when I met them," Kyra responded, "a happy family, living a simple life because they didn't know anything else, and then one day they were pushed out to allow for those monstrosities you see there now."

"Sorry to hear that. I know the Afghani people are proud, so maybe you can find some way to compensate them for helping us that won't insult their beliefs."

"They are proud people. They don't have much, but will offer it up to strangers in a heartbeat. I am just as concerned with protecting them. If the Taliban or insurgents discover a family of Afghani's are helping the *Infidels*, they will take off their heads."

"Which is why they should accept our help," Brady said. "We should be out of here soon, if Hadley's time frame was accurate."

Less than a few minutes later, he tapped her on the arm. "Show time," he said, "Looks like Hadley's timing was right on."

"Two dark-colored Toyota Land Cruisers with blackened-out windows, and I'm guessing armored with bullet-proof glass, just passed through a security checkpoint by rolling down the window and allowing security to see who was inside; headed toward the Sherpur District."

Kyra refocused her binoculars and zoomed in.

CHAPTER 8

Dalton LeClair studied the terrain through the scope mounted on his Remington M24 sniper rifle. Wearing a desert camo ghillie suit he was invisible to the average eye, perched on a platform between a mulberry bush and the bombed out remnants of what used to be an Afghani family's mud brick home. Twigs with mud and dirt packed around his desert netting hid the muzzle of his rifle. From his location, there were no obstructions in his path; it was just a matter of getting the targets in his crosshairs then taking the shot.

Before the trip to Afghanistan, he scouted the area through satellite images, viewing them at different times of the day to see who came and went, looking for abandoned properties. He arrived undercover, dressed as a goat herder walking through the streets of Kabul, circling and doubling back several times before winding up at his designation.

He had reservations about this contract. In truth, he questioned every hit his boss hired him to do, but with exception to one, they were disgruntled drug dealers, rival arms dealers, or buyers trying to double-cross him once the deal was completed. According to his boss, if they were involved in the business, they knew the score.

This contract seemed vague. Cryptic messages, delivered in a manner fitting of the cold war, a dead drop alerting him to a hit, two players, but no hint as to whom. A big fan of those days, his boss used tricks from the KGB to pass along messages, ideas he often picked from watching old spy thrillers.

He didn't set out to be an assassin; his skills with a rifle guided him down that lonely road. He was at a shooting range in Miami, Florida a few years ago when a young, rich guy approached him. The guy didn't offer a name, just a business card with a job offer. He painted an innocent picture; he was looking for a bodyguard to handle security on his Yacht, where he conducted most of his business. There would be traveling, exotic locations, and the money would be good.

Just past the drinking age, Dalton was looking for adventure. He had no family to keep him in Miami. The foster parents who raised him died in a car accident when he was nineteen. The fact that the guy didn't cough up a name was strange, but it was Miami, there was a lot of strange. After weighing the pros and cons, he jumped at the gig.

To train him for the job, the guy sent him to a private boot camp run by former members of Delta Force. Over a six-month period, they turned him into a machine, instructing him in survival, reconnaissance and surveillance, defensive driving and boating maneuvers, martial arts for his own protection, and the ways of a sniper. He already knew his way around weapons—he was hunting gators in the swamps at the age of five—but with what he learned at the camp, he was golden.

The week after boot camp, he learned the truth. He wasn't hired to be a personal bodyguard; he was hired to be an assassin. Using dead drop techniques, the guy provided orders for the first hit.

LeClair declined.

In retaliation, hooded men kidnapped him from his bed and took him to an underground location, where they strung him up to the ceiling by his wrists and chained his ankles to the floor. They left him alone for the next forty-eight hours with no food or water, and only a table filled with torture tools to think about.

On the third day, another hooded man appeared with a knife sheathed to his thigh, while what his new boss sat on a chair, one leg crossed over the other, casually smoking a cigar. Another man in a suit stood in the shadows, watching, but not allowing his identity to be known.

The hooded man tortured him using rubber hoses, repeated hits to the body, and stun guns rendering him unconscious, only to revive him, and begin again. His new boss would intervene and play the role of the devoted friend, providing sips of water, rice, and bread. Day after day the routine continued.

It took several months before LeClair reached his breaking point, and succumbed to their wishes. When his boss offered him a chance to redeem himself, and finally be free, LeClair agreed. They nursed him back to health. The only physical scar remaining was a knife wound across his cheek—one that the hooded man delivered in a fit of rage when LeClair remained defiant, but the hoses and stun guns inflicted internal damage that were forever in his psyche.

Then like a master leading its protégé, his boss set up another dead drop message, wired two-hundred-thousand dollars into an offshore account, and LeClair, grudgingly, made his first human kill.

By noon the next day, another payment was wired to his account, and a newspaper was delivered to the marina where he had his boat docked. The front-page showed the dead body of the man he killed, and the article indicated that he was a 'wanted man' in two countries for his involvement with extremists.

The knowledge that his first kill was not an innocent bystander gave LeClair a feeling of relief.

That set the trend for the love/hate relationship between master and assassin over the next few years. The master would initiate contact through dead drop locations. LeClair had so many days to respond. If he was late, the hooded man inevitably appeared—how they knew where he was, he did not know. The song and dance continued until LeClair no longer contested, mainly because his kills, so far, had been less than reputable individuals, and he convinced himself that it was their fault for choosing the wrong side of the law.

Once he was under their thumb, he finally learned the identities of the hooded man and the master, and so became the ongoing relationship. The suit in the shadows was the only identity he was yet to discover.

Dead drops, emails, pre-paid cell phones, occasional invitations to important gatherings and parties, gave the illusion that he was trusted. With no family of his own, he felt somewhat of an alliance, but inevitably, he was only there for the kill.

LeClair had to admit he loved the money. The price was greater for high-profile-individuals, and he enjoyed the lifestyle of traveling, and being able to afford all that he desired. Hanging out at marinas in Miami, he always wanted his own Yacht. As long as the targets were corrupt—which most of them were—he could justify his actions.

Yet, no matter whom the intended targets were, whether they deserved it, or not, he still longed for the day when he could break away for good, and he wondered if that day was closer than he realized.

What was it about this new contract that made him take pause? Nothing I can do about it, now.

Looking through the viewfinder, he continued his search for the targets, combing over the location sent to him in a text message that morning.

CHAPTER 9

The Land Cruisers passed the concrete barriers protecting the neighborhood, and drove past row after row of garish, multi-storied homes, stacked side by side described architecturally as 'Narco-Tecture'—one of them built to resemble the White House, only red in color with the same white pillars.

The convoy arrived at its destination, a five-story palace built right up against the hills. With colors resembling that of a Mexican Hacienda, the large mansion took up two city blocks, had close to sixty rooms, a nightclub built in an underground basement with secret tunnel entrances, and the garage was large enough to handle over fifty vehicles.

Cash stepped out of the front-passenger seat of the leading Land Cruiser, and casually glanced around while taking a moment to light his Cigar. He stood about five-feet-eleven, slender with a swimmer's body. Sandy-blond hair, cut short and styled like that of a GQ cover model, he was dressed in the type of casual attire one would see on a Yacht moored off the Caribbean; khaki shorts, buttoned-down silk shirt, and deck shoes, even though the temperature was a bit on the cool side.

He was not armed, but then again, he didn't need to be. He paid big money to various sources: Politicians,

59

Military Officials, Afghan security personnel, the Taliban, insurgents and private contractors, which afforded him the luxury of conducting business without interference.

On trips to Afghanistan, Pakistan, and other Middle-East locations, he always traveled with his driver, Donghai, an Asian fluent in martial arts, and his right-hand man whom he referred to as The Chechen, where he was born and trained. Hearing that, oddly enough, usually caused adversaries to hesitate when dealing with him.

There were rumors that Osama Bin Laden—the most wanted terrorist in the world before a team of Navy SEALs took him out—had Chechen bodyguards when traveling. Chechen mercs had a reputation for being vicious, even boasting that one Chechen was equal to ten mercs of any other nationality.

Donghai stepped out from the driver's seat, wearing dark fatigues and a pair of Oakley sunglasses, but remained by the vehicle like a dutiful servant.

The Chechen followed up from the back seat, but took a position next to his boss. As he did, his cruel eyes took in the surroundings. He was dressed in charcoal, gray army fatigues, sleeves rolled up on his arms, revealing the tattoo of a wolf—the token symbol of his country—a knife sheathed on his thigh, and armed with a Kalashnikov rifle.

***

When the development of Sherpur took shape, Cash purchased land under the name of one of his private corporations then hired an architect to design a home to his specifications, and rented it out for profits to NGOs aiding in the rebuilding efforts. Once the lease expired at the end of 2013 and no other takers due to the talks of troops leaving Afghanistan at the end of 2014, he added various security measures to what he already had in place.

After the home was vacant, he had the original architect design a cave inside the hill behind the opulent home with steel doors at the exit points, and dimensions large enough for a large truck to drive through to drop off and collect supplies. He also wanted the design to fit into the desert landscape, away from probing eyes through satellite surveillance over Afghanistan. The final touch was a 3-D mural design of a desert landscape, painted onto the doors, so viewers would have no idea there was an opening into the hill.

Similar to caves used by *Osama Bin Laden* and the Taliban up in the mountains of Afghanistan, the cave consisted of two floors with rooms large enough to conduct business and store supplies, and was also wired for lighting, power, and a ventilation system. Inside, he could access the internet and watch Satellite TV. Unlike the rumors of Bin Laden's caves, there were no tunnels or escape routes to Pakistan. Cash didn't spend much time in Afghanistan; only when he needed to conduct business, and on those occasions he procured the necessary precautions—bribes, security, etc.—in advance of the trips.

As if on cue, a white Toyota Tacoma Truck pulled up behind them. The vehicle looked like it traveled directly through the war zone, packed with mud and dirt, bullet holes down the center of the driver's door and blood was splattered across the bed. Following it up in the rear was a silver Land Rover, also with tinted windows and armored for protection.

Thomas Hadley jumped out of the passenger seat of the Tacoma Truck, looking like a teenager eager to meet his idol. He carried his silver attaché case at his side, and a smile plastered across his face. Enamored by the mega rich gunrunner, he strode toward Cash with his hand extended.

Like a coiled snake ready to strike, The Chechen stepped in front of him to intercede and kept him from getting close to his boss.

The driver's side door of the Tacoma banged open as Fuchs jumped out and rushed to Hadley's side, ready to protect the man who kept the tax-free money flowing. He wore an armored vest, an ammo belt with extra magazines wrapped around it, and carried an M-4; causing an intense standoff between the two bodyguards.

"It's all right," Cash said with a dismissive hand toward The Chechen, who reluctantly returned to his position alongside his boss.

Fuchs stepped back as well, but kept his eyes firmly planted on The Chechen, assuming he was more of a threat than anyone else at the meeting.

Cash returned the handshake with Hadley. "Welcome, Mr. Hadley. You'll have to excuse my bodyguard. He gets a little overeager at times, whereas my driver has the capacity to remain as still as a corpse." There was a brief glance, possibly one of distrust, between the two.

"I appreciate you coming here. Once again, you have proven yourself to be a loyal asset, even if that loyalty is at a huge cost."

Hadley suppressed a smile, knowing any retort could get him shot. Both men fell silent as three armed men in traditional Afghan clothing stepped out of the Land Rover with their AK-47s slung over their shoulder.

The driver, a man only known as Ahmed, scanned the area in a highly skilled manner, while the others took up offensive positions. With a nod from Ahmed, the back seat door opened and Tariq Jaffri stepped out.

Standing at five-foot-six, dark hair and skin, with wire-framed glasses and wearing a tailored suit, he could have passed for a university professor.

He was born and raised in Pakistan, until he turned thirteen when his father moved the family to Michigan, where he owned several convenient stores. He adapted well to living in the United States; he attended the local Mosque and had many friends. When he graduated high school, he went on to get a degree in business at the University of Michigan. In his mid-twenties, he moved to New York to buy his own chain of convenient stores, and purchased a home in the heart of Manhattan. Life was great, until the troops invaded Afghanistan.

Thoughts of hatred toward the United States didn't form overnight. He started spending time online, searching for websites and forums looking for others that shared his views. He traveled back to Pakistan, spending time with young men, just like him. They visited a camp, which intensified his anger, but when he returned to New York, he didn't know what he could do.

That all changed the day he saw a news report, declaring that a team of Navy SEALs killed Osama Bin Laden—a man he idolized. From that day on, Jaffri declared that he would do whatever he could to help the Taliban and al Qaeda insurgents defeat the enemy.

If they needed weapons, he would supply them.

If they needed transportation, he would get it.

If they needed missiles, IEDs, grenades and explosives, he would find them.

And if they needed a continuous supply of money, he would raise it.

It would be done.

Hadley said, "Cash, may I present Tariq Jaffri."

Always affable, Cash offered his hand, which Jaffri accepted while never changing his serious demeanor.

"Mr. Jaffri, I hope this will be the beginning of a prosperous relationship," Cash said. "Shall we go inside?"

Cash glanced toward the second Land Cruiser and gave a perfunctory nod toward the henchmen remaining inside. Dressed in dark fatigues, four locals exited the vehicles and stood by for further instructions.

"Who are they?" Jaffri demanded.

"They are merely hired hands," Cash said, ignoring the worried look on Jaffri's face. "You will see."

Cash directed a remote control toward the 3-D mural. The men watched in stunned amazement as the steel doors began to slide open.

"I am sorry," Jaffri interrupted, "but before we proceed any further, I must have my men check for wires or transmitters."

For the first time, Cash showed displeasure. His jaw clenched. "Ah, a cautious man," he said, and then he caught himself and smiled. "I understand."

"Assume the worst, you live longer." Jaffri stated.

Cash gave him a half nod. "Of course, proceed."

Jaffri's expression remained passive, while Ahmed proceeded to frisk each man, even those that were merely 'hired hands'. Once he finished, everyone followed Cash, who glanced toward the hills one more time and smiled, just before he disappeared inside.

CHAPTER 10

"**Intel was right,**" Brady said, from his spot buried in the sand. "With all the firepower the bodyguards are carrying, this is definitely a meeting worth viewing."

Glued to their binoculars, Kyra and Brady focused their eyes on the men who showed up to the meeting down below.

"Guess bringing criminal elements together is financially lucrative," Kyra said, in a mocking tone. "Did Tin get an I.D. on the big wig yet?"

"The guy has a few aliases, but the name on his birth certificate is Colton Cash Tate, so he's been going by his middle name. Not much is known about his early years, yet. Wound up at the University of Miami, Florida when he was eighteen."

"Not exactly tops on the list of American Universities."

"From what I gather, his interests were more in line with the Miami nightlife," Brady said.

Kyra chuckled. "Ah, so his idea of higher education was topless girls on spring break taking exotic drugs?"

"Isn't that the American way?"

"Speaking from your own experiences?"

Brady paused and smiled, as if remembering earlier times. "That was a lifetime before I married the woman of my dreams, and became the father of twin girls, who I hope to steer clear of the wild spring break escapades."

Kyra returned the smile. "I saw their pictures on your desk. They're adorable. Lucky for you they didn't get your mug."

"Thankfully, they take after their mother in the looks department. But back to the matter at hand," Brady said, changing the subject while he snatched a Canon EOS 5D Mark III digital camera from his gear. He didn't like discussing his family out in the field, choosing to reserve those discussions for the safe house, or when they were home on American soil. His girls were innocent and pure, and he always wanted to think of them in that way—hard to do on a mission dealing with what he perceived to be the scum of the earth.

"This guy, Cash, was smart," he said, as he adjusted the zoom in capabilities on the camera while fixing on the images down below, and then started snapping pictures. "His freshman year at the university, he started a construction company buying fixer-uppers, renovating them using illegals who couldn't complain about wages, and then flipping them. He made huge profits, which he poured into the stock market and other businesses then wound up with a fortune. By the time he graduated, he was already a multi-millionaire. Now, he owns real estate in locations all over the world; has three Yachts, several personal vehicles, and a fleet of SUVs. He is also the owner of a Formula 1 race car and a team of drivers."

Kyra whistled to herself, but sarcastically added, "Bet he always has a pretty-young-thing dangling on each arm too. Probably a new one in every port—the type of woman who doesn't ask questions, as long as he keeps supplying her with the goods."

"Why do you think it's so enticing for young soldiers to farm themselves out for security details after they return from war? The kind of money they can make protecting some of these yahoos, offers a much better lifestyle for the future than a job at *Walmart* or *Home Depot*—which are two companies doing their best to hire veterans returning from war. On paper, this guy comes off as a young, wealthy businessman."

"On paper, yes," Kyra said, "but that guy he's got protecting him right now; he's no American soldier."

Brady said, "From what Tin could piece together, I.G.R. was started by bidding for weapons at online auctions, and then winning out the contracts from government and state agencies. For years, most of the deals were legal and by the book. Apparently, the illegal weapons deals were turning out to bring in huge profits, so he, or they—depending on who else is behind the company—explored more. Who knows, maybe Cash got a taste of the power and prefers the illegal lifestyle more than the legitimate one. For some, it can turn into a form of addiction. It is a stretch to assume an individual who makes a living buy and selling real estate, would ultimately wind up as an International arms dealer, but the way Cash passed through the security checkpoint, it's obvious he has a lot of people in his pocket.

"That's probably how he stayed off the radar for so long," Kyra said. She mulled over the information, while focusing the binoculars directly on Cash. It surprised her that he was so young, probably late twenties, early thirties, and dressed as if he was going sailing, not in a war-torn area making an illegal weapons deal. Her immediate reaction of him was that he was arrogant; something that wouldn't be picked up in Intelligence reports. She guessed he was a man who needed to be in control and would not take kindly to the word no. The fact that he didn't carry a weapon also told her that he didn't think he would ever be caught.

"Okay, so what's our end game?" Kyra said. "What do we know about the buyer?"

"That's what this recon is all about; we need to find out."

"So we observe, but don't interfere. I got that, but we're not going to get much up here. Maybe we should go in for a closer look, see if we can't pick up on their voices and hear what's going down?"

"Way ahead of you," Brady said, "I'm senior here, I'll go. You stay here and watch my six."

"Copy that," she said, "but don't give me shit if the Victoria Secret gals reconvene their photo shoot and you miss out, once again."

"I'll save that image for later." He grabbed his Digital Desert Backpack from the trench they dug in the sand to hide everything, quickly checked his gear, and placed the camera back inside then took a quick drink from his CamelBak.

After a mock salute to Kyra, he crab-walked out of the sand and slowly departed from their location, staying down low behind rocks, bushes and debris on the hill, and doing his best to remain out of sight from those down below.

CHAPTER 11

Wall-to-wall shelves lined the first floor of the cave, stockpiled with cargoes and crates made to look like supplies for the ICRC—International Red Cross. Ahmed walked the perimeter with a magnetic wand, also checking the cave for wires while Cash stood by wearing a fake smile.

He did not take kindly to the treatment of mistrust by someone whom he considered beneath him. He had little respect for those who aligned themselves with the Taliban and insurgents; though he didn't care about their cause, for him, it was all about the money and nothing more.

No matter, he thought to himself, this was the only time he would have to meet with Jaffri. During the initial talks it was agreed that future transactions could be made online with the money wired to an account of his choice—like most of his other deals—and delivery of the product would be made per the arrangements agreed upon in advance.

Once Ahmed gave the all clear, Jaffri turned toward Cash, and said, "Where are my weapons?"

Cash raised his eyebrows at the tone and motioned toward the briefcase. "You have the first payment?"

Jaffri handed him the leather briefcase.

Cash walked over toward a crate, set the briefcase on top and opened it. Inside were stacks of one-hundred-dollar bills. Cash nodded to The Chechen, and he walked over and proceeded to count the money, and verify that it was not counterfeit.

Cash normally insisted transactions be completed by funds being wired to an account, whether he was the one paying or receiving. This deal was the exception, since it was a first-time meeting, and because the weapons would be winding up in the hands of insurgents. Trust was an issue.

"Surely you must know I would not cheat you," Jaffri said, as he waved his hand around, mildly irritated. "Here in the middle of the desert, where could I go?"

Cash proffered a sarcastic smile. "Assume the worst, you'll never be cheated," he said, using some of Jaffri's own words against him.

Jaffri was not amused.

Once The Chechen completed his check of the funds, he handed the briefcase back to Cash, who in turn, removed several stacks of bills and handed them to Hadley. "For your continued loyalty."

"Pleasure doing business with you," Hadley said. Elated, he stacked the money into his silver attaché case, and prepared to remove himself from the premises. He shook hands with each of the men then Fuchs walked them back toward the Tacoma, with his weapon at the ready and prepared to shoot, until they were safely inside, driving out of the Sherpur District.

With them out of the area, Cash pulled out a radio and issued an order. Seconds later, a large white truck with the ICRC logo painted on the sides and hood, pulled out from the back of the cave. Two guards hopped out from behind the driver and passenger seat, and walked over toward one of the crates along the wall.

Using a crowbar, they removed the top of the first crate, and stepped aside for Jaffri to look inside. Lying underneath several first aid kits and medical supplies were boxes of dry food products of rice and grains. Safely hidden among the rice and grains, Jaffri discovered neatly packaged bags of Opium—with a colorful logo of Palm Trees and a gator on the front.

"The American military can't even stop the poppy fields," Jaffri said with amusement.

Cash shrugged. "Who said they're trying?"

Removing the lids from the two remaining crates, Jaffri's face became animated to see various weapons stacked inside, camouflaged in the same manner as the Opium; R.P.G.'s with launcher tubes, IEDs, AK-47's, M-16s, Mortars, and pallets of ammunition.

Jaffri said, "Praise Allah. My friends will be pleased."

"I'm sure they're looking forward to Paradise," Cash said, doing his best to remain aloof. He was a supplier of weapons, and tried not to engage in the discussions of war. Each side had their own interpretation for what they believed was right, which more often than not involved religion, but he really didn't care. Money was his religion.

"You've made arrangements at the checkpoints?"

"You paid me to do so," Cash said. He motioned toward the logo on the truck. "And with a painted red cross on top of the truck, NATO surveillance or American Drones will identify it as a vehicle for the ICRC when traveling to its destination."

Wearing a malevolent grin, Jaffri said, "Good, let the Americans explain how their weapons are killing their own troops and Afghani civilians. Ahmed, if you would be so kind." Jaffri motioned to his driver.

Ahmed walked over toward the first crate, lifted one of the tiny bags of Opium from the box of dry food, and proceeded to inspect the product. With a nod of approval toward Jaffri, the two of them joined Cash at the back of the truck.

"I'm sure this is what you've been waiting to see," Cash said, as he nodded to his men to pull back the canvas on the truck to reveal pallets containing surface-to-air missiles.

Jaffri gasped. "American," he said, with a snide smile as his eyes lit up. "Are those missiles part of the 400 rumored to have been stolen from Libya?"

Cash merely shrugged. "Where they come from is not something you should concern yourself with. Now, you have seen the product, so we have completed the first part of the transaction as discussed. Perhaps we should wrap things up, before our luck runs out."

Jaffri nodded, appeased, but then his eyes took on a hardened glaze. "Once I receive word from my fellow insurgents that the weapons are in their hands, you can expect the next payment into your account as agreed via the original discussion. However, final payment will not be made until delivery of the Opium is received in the states, as per your agreement."

"I didn't build a successful business by going back on my word," Cash said, keeping his face devoid of any expression as he motioned to his men to start loading the crates.

Ahmed escorted Jaffri back to the Land Rover. His other guards followed and they all took their respective seats. As the Land Rover pulled away from the area, Cash turned toward The Chechen.

"I think our friend Jaffri might need a little more scrutinizing."

The Chechen smiled.

CHAPTER 12

With the players inside the cave and out of her eyesight, Kyra kept the binoculars zoomed in and focused on Brady. He buried himself under a pile of rubbish, about one-hundred-yards away from their original position toward the bottom of the hill, close enough to capture the faces of the men at the meeting as they came and went, but still remaining out of their sight.

Her eyes combed over the area doing a quick 360-degree scan of the terrain to see if all was clear. Other than the members of ATU, nobody knew they were in the area, so there shouldn't be anyone observing them. Still, in a war zone there was always someone doing surveillance, so she would be remiss not to keep a watchful eye.

That's when she saw something. Approximately 300 meters from her location; downwind, she spotted a herd of goats eating the bitter desert plants, hovering near a block of abandoned mud brick homes down near the Kabul River.

One home in particular was dilapidated—the roof and side blown off—the result of a mortar or bomb blast, either from the current war, or left over from the days of the Soviets. Twigs and branches nestled all around.

A sudden movement sent a chill down her spine.

There wasn't much of a breeze, so that wasn't the cause. Was it a goat that got separated from its herd, or a critter? She did a quick sweep around the homes; other than the goats, it was clear.

Zooming back in, she analyzed the twigs and branches of the brush, and then her military training kicked in and she realized what she was seeing: a ghillie suit and desert netting.

A sniper!

Frantic, she magnified her view. Yep, dammit, it was definitely a sniper. She saw the pointed end of the muzzle of the rifle ... aimed directly toward Brady.

Her heart leapt up in her throat as she kicked into high gear. "Brady, get your ass down," she yelled into the mic. "There's a sniper!"

She positioned the binoculars back on Brady just in time to see him throwing the backpack over his shoulder, turn in her direction and start to crab-walk back.

She yelled, again. "Brady, hit the dirt! There's a sniper down in a mud hut and he's got you in his crosshairs. Take cover! I repeat, take cover!"

At the same time Brady was hearing her words through his earpiece, he instinctively looked toward the collection of mud huts to confirm the threat. A momentary flash of shock settled over his face, right before a bullet ripped into his forehead, shattered his skull and sent blood and brain matter flying before his body slumped to the ground.

"Fuck! ... Oh Brady..."

Horrified and devastated, Kyra tried to remain focused. She couldn't stay there. She was a target too! It was up to her to complete the op, but right now she wanted to scream and wrap her hands around the throat of the sniper. Brady had a wife and two kids.

It was supposed to be a simple case of recon. Only a small number of people knew they were even in the country.

So who the hell wanted them dead?

She gathered her gear and jumped to her feet. He only needed one shot. Running as if her life depended on it, because it did, she raced down the hill toward Brady's body. She veered this way and that, staying down low, trying to avoid being a moving target.

Kyra knew Brady was dead. She had been in a war zone, and seen a few headshots. There wasn't anything she could do. Now, it was her responsibility to get the camera and remove anything on his body that might identity him in case someone found the body before she could get him home.

She had been a runner in high school and maintained her speed through the years, so it only took her a short time to reach his body. With tears flowing down her cheek, she grabbed his backpack, checked each pocket and removed his wedding ring that he taped to the interior of his tactical vest. They were supposed to leave personal items at home, but Brady said he needed it close by. She didn't want to leave him, but she had no choice. Until she could return, she covered him with the desert netting, and slipped his backpack over her other shoulder. She stood up and started down the hill.

The bullet hit her on the left center of the chest, knocking her back from the power of the impact. It felt like her lungs were exploding as she struggled to breathe, and she slowly lost consciousness.

A few moments later, her eyes popped open and she jackknifed back up. "Son-of-a...," she gritted through clenched teeth. The pain was unbearable.

Then she realized that the heavy-duty armor plate she wore over her vest helped to see her through another day. The bullet blasted into the ceramic plate, cracking it, but it did not pass through the second layer of Kevlar.

Struggling to breathe, she realized her ribs were sore, possibly cracked, or at the very least bruised, but she couldn't stay still, she had to keep moving. This was not how she wanted her life to end—a sniper bullet on a desert, caught unaware during a simple case of surveillance—not here, not now. Dammit to hell, that's not how Brady should have died either.

She didn't have time to remove the vest; her mind was telling her to get back on her feet, so she struggled through the pain and forced her feet to move. Judging by the location of the entry of the bullet, she knew the assassin was moving too.

She started jogging, her long legs gliding over the sand, one foot in front of the other, until she could get her breathing back on track. Once she could feel the air come through her lungs and let it out through her nose without feeling the need to scream out in pain, she picked up the speed. Running now, pumping her arms to give her the momentum to go faster.

She reminded herself of Tin and J.D.'s words back at ops: she was on an unsanctioned surveillance mission. She was on her own. No military forces were coming in to save the day. No other operatives.

She needed to get to the safe house.

When she cleared the bottom of the hill, she cut behind a building to get the lay of the land.

The meet and greet was in the Sherpur District to her left. The assassin took his shots from an area off to the right. Where he was now, she had no clue.

The decision made, she cut down an alley going straight through the center. Running through garbage, debris and dodging craters and potholes in the streets, she kept going. Her eyes swept left then right and she listened for sounds behind her.

A few blocks later, she cut down another alley to the right, then a quick left, which took her through a row of mud-brick homes.

Then she heard it.

Feet pounded the gravel and mud pavement behind her. She darted a glance over her shoulder, a man in a robe and urban mask was chasing after her. He didn't have a sniper rifle, but he had a pistol. No idea what brand. She wanted to keep moving, not see the brand of gun that was going to shoot her. He wasn't firing at her, yet. She assumed that was to avoid the attention. She knew that could change.

She cut to the left, hustled through someone's back yard—dodging between the rugs hanging on clotheslines. Once she reached the street, she darted in between a row of buses that looked like they were waiting for repairs; there were dents, bullet-shattered windows, and missing hubcaps and tires.

No longer hearing footsteps behind her, she peaked around the final bus before rushing out in the open; the robed man was nowhere around. Breathing a little easier, she continued running, but tripped over a pile of debris in the road, and fell to her knees, skinning them in the process.

She picked herself back up and ran a few more feet, pausing again to allow a young boy leading a herd of goats to pass to the opposite side of the road. Fearing the assassin would get the chance to catch up to her, she pushed the last remaining goats out of the way—getting a nasty look from the young boy.

"Sorry," she yelled in Pashto.

She ran several more blocks, rounded the corner—the safe house a few more streets away—and, literally, ran into the assassin. An open palm slammed into her head, knocking her for a loop. As she slowly dropped to the ground, he aimed his weapon to her forehead, and she prepared to say goodbye.

Their eyes locked sending a surge of heat and adrenaline through both of them, but instead of pulling the trigger, Dalton LeClair stared at her with a puzzled expression, pulled the traditional scarf away from her face, and let out an audible gasp.

Troubled and confused by the situation, but not having a clear answer as to why, the next thing he did was to mumble, "I'm sorry."

That was the last thing she heard before she lost consciousness, once again.

In robotic mode, LeClair secured his weapon. Underneath the robe, he was wearing desert BDUs, and a tactical vest with pockets. He rifled through the backpacks she was carrying until he found the camera, and stored it in one of the vest pockets, leaving everything else intact. Out of the corner of his eye, he noticed a local Afghani man, woman, and young girl watching him. He had to move. Knowing she wouldn't be out for long, he headed back to the Sherpur District for his scheduled rendezvous.

By the time he returned to the cave, Cash was finishing up with his hired help, explaining paperwork and giving final instructions for delivering the trucks filled with weapons to their new location. Once the vehicles pulled away from the area—one truck going in the opposite direction with a nod from Cash—then he, LeClair and The Chechen joined the driver, Donghai, back in the Land Cruiser.

"Can I assume my pest problem has been taken care of?" Cash said to LeClair, analyzing his reaction with probing eyes.

LeClair gave him a perfunctory nod as he handed over the camera. He had no intention of admitting he could not take the final shot. If he did, Cash would just send The Chechen to fulfill the order. The woman would probably be tortured in ways that LeClair remembered all too well, and in ways no woman should ever be subjected to, then things would be messy for both of them, and ultimately end with their demise.

He wouldn't allow that. No. Better to have Cash believe the two individuals were no longer a problem. He would deal with the fallout later, when the truth revealed itself—and he knew it would—but on his own turf and not in the desert of Afghanistan.

"Very well," Cash said with a tone of irritation in his voice, "then let's get the hell out of here. I'm tired of constantly rubbing sand from my eyes."

Cash directed the remote toward the 3-D desert image, and the steel doors closed behind them.

CHAPTER 13

Washington, D.C.

Several days later, the wheels of a C-130 cargo plane touched down on the runway at the Dulles International Airport in Washington D.C., and rolled to a stop.

Kyra's colleagues from ATU, CO Barry West, Tin Tran and J.D. Gibson waited on the tarmac next to a dark-colored sedan and a vehicle from the Morgue, with its drivers standing by waiting.

Minutes passed before the ramp lowered and Kyra walked down the back, rucksacks slung over her shoulders, and her head down, visibly shaken. She was dressed in a black BDU shirt and pant, with jump boots, her hair pulled back in a ponytail.

Tin and J.D. walked up to her, took the load off her shoulders, and each of them gave her a hug.

West followed, and shook her hand. The four of them then turned around and focused their attention on the aircraft. Standing stoically, they watched as four young soldiers lowered a casket down the ramp holding the body of Mike Brady, and then loaded it into the back of the waiting vehicle.

As Kyra stepped into the back seat of the sedan, she couldn't help but reflect on the last few days, and realized how lucky she was to come back alive. She owed her life to the Afghani family.

***

Dawood, Hadiah, and Sadia had witnessed the death of Brady; then saw her running down the hill in an effort to escape. They were horrified when a bullet ripped into her body; thinking she was dead. When they saw her wake up moments later, they followed her through the streets, keeping in the shadows. Seeing the robed man chasing after her, they ducked out of sight. By the time they came back out, she was gone. The boy herding the goats led them to her.

At great risk to their family, they covered her from head to toe and carried her back to their tent. If anyone discovered them helping her, word would quickly spread through the streets of Kabul, and eventually, the Taliban or insurgents would learn of their treachery. They would surely have been killed, but brutally tortured beforehand to send a message to others.

Back at their tent, Hadia and Sadia tried to keep her comfortable, feeding her what little food they had, while Dawood risked his life trying to get word to the military. Kyra already knew they wouldn't send anyone. In the end, it was her Uncle Ray who got wind of her absence, and raised holy hell.

A day later, a convoy of Humvees from the Bagram Air Base dispatched to make the rescue and recover the body of Mike Brady. Kyra was indebted and would be forever grateful to the Afghani family, and would do whatever she could to help them, even though she knew they might be too proud to accept.

CHAPTER 14

Langley, Virginia

"Who the hell was in charge of this colossal cluster fuck?" Jack Thompson shouted, asking the question more interested in striking fear than actually getting a response, considering he already knew the answer from reading the report that was sitting in front of him.

Kyra and her superior, Barry West of ATU, sat directly across the mahogany conference table from Jack Thompson and Marty Sanger, both members of the National Clandestine Service tasked with overseeing the unit behind the scenes in D.C.

A large flat-screen monitor hung on the wall at the head of the table displaying satellite images of the area surrounding the Sherpur District and Colton Cash Tate's man-made cave.

Kyra and West remained quiet, not offering an answer to the question. Before arriving at the meeting, West informed her that they would try to bait her, and that she should just answer questions pertaining to the op, period.

"Why don't we start with why the two of you were even in the area?" Marty Sanger said, offering the trace of a smile to put her at ease. Sanger was a former prosecutor in New York known for his involvement in high-profile mob-related trials, and a good friend to

87

former Mayor Rudy Giuliani. He had his suit jacket off, his sleeves rolled up, and two bottles of water stood next to his stack of files that he obsessively drank from to keep from getting dehydrated.

Kyra glanced toward Barry who nodded his consent.

"We're all friends here, Miss Ray," Thompson interrupted upon seeing her hesitation. "You don't need his permission to speak.

Barry West gave Jack Thompson a scathing glance. "Let's be clear; we are only in here because you pitched a hissy fit that we didn't advise you of this op in the first place. She'll proceed when she's goddamn ready."

Noticing his tone, Kyra wondered if these two had a past history together, or if the animosity she detected in their voices was just political in nature. "I'm ready."

"Then by all means, proceed."

"Mike Brady received a communication from one of his assets in Afghanistan that he was contacted to broker an arms deal between two major players. Intel suggested that the weapons could wind up in the hands of the Taliban and insurgents with plans to use them against troops and innocent westerners. We wanted to know who the players were, see if we could get more info regarding the deal, so we were in the area on a reconnaissance mission—strictly surveillance."

Thompson's face turned beat red—one of the symptoms from his high blood pressure and cholesterol count resulting from too much stress on the job. He glared at Kyra with a look of skepticism. "Since when does surveillance wind up with one agent dead?"

Jack Thompson was known as a pit bull in the arena of SOOs, which also didn't help with his health issues. He earned the nickname from his time as a Detective in Virginia. His idea of getting answers was to go on the attack right out of the gate then ease off later, when he had to make nice. That was how he wound up with the highest conviction rate in Roanoke, Virginia, and ultimately helped in cutting down crime in the city.

Feeling the sting of eyes and suspicion, Kyra gathered her wits about her. "Brady was attempting to get a visual of the subjects, and went in for a closer look to take pictures for our tech guy to analyze."

"Ah yes," Sanger said, sarcastically, "the infamous camera that doesn't seem to exist."

"Are you calling me a liar?" Kyra demanded. "I told you the assassin confiscated it when he chased me through the streets of Kabul. That's in the report."

Thompson and Sanger shared a look. "Yes," Thompson said with skepticism, "that was your story. We just find it suspect to say the least."

"Your story notwithstanding, what we've got is a botched operation—"

Thompson interrupted. "One that was not authorized, I might add. Why were we not read in on this operation?"

"I signed off on it," Barry West said, irritated that they were wasting time. "If I'm not mistaken, I have the authority to manage my people without having to run to you every time I need to wipe my ass. As far as I'm concerned, reconnaissance and surveillance missions are not the type of ops that need the approval of committees."

"That may be Barry, but tell us how we're supposed to explain the end result. No tangible Intel, and a widow with two young daughters," Sanger added for effect.

Kyra grimaced. "Sir, the death of Mike Brady is regrettable, and will haunt me for the rest of my life. He was a colleague and my friend, but I don't believe the operation was botched, and he would want me to see it through. As you can see our analysts, Tin Tran and J.D. Gibson, now have the area under surveillance," she said referring to the satellite images. "And--"

Thompson interrupted by waving a dismissive hand toward her then glanced at a document in front of him. "I understand you lost your parents in the terrorist attack on September 11, 2001? This meeting aside, let me take a moment to offer our condolences to you. Our nation suffered a terrible loss that day."

"They were passengers on Flight 77," Barry West said, realizing they were touching on a sensitive area.

"I would also like to extend our gratitude for your service to this country. We were all praying for your safe return when it was discovered you were being held captive by insurgents during your time with the military."

"Thank you," Kyra said in a soft voice, but she was immediately on guard. For them to bring up personal information, she didn't think she was going to like what was coming next.

"Your uncle also works closely with the president, is that right?" Sanger asked her pointedly.

Observing West out of the corner of her eye, Kyra noticed he was glancing down at the papers in front of him, but underneath the table his hand softly tapped her on the arm. She was sure that was his way of telling her to keep it cool, and not let these piss-ants—his favorite word—get under her skin.

Kyra focused her attention on Marty Sanger. "Yes, you could say my Uncle Ray is on a friendly basis with President Davis. I believe they get together a couple times a year to do a ride for wounded vets, and another weekend they take part in a golf tournament that also raises funds for charities involving the military. What the hell does my family history have to do with this?"

Thompson gave her a pointed stare. "Causes us to question how you became a junior operative with ATU at such a young age; and were afforded the opportunity for fieldwork right off the bat. Were strings pulled on your behalf—favors granted?"

Dismayed, Kyra stood up and placed both hands on the table, looking them both in the eyes. "Excuse me, but Mike Brady is dead because a billionaire who hides behind his legitimate businesses is selling weapons, drugs, and god knows what else to the highest

91

bidders—weapons that are being used to kill American troops and other innocents. Moreover, he obviously hired an assassin to take out anyone who gets in his way. I would think you'd want us out there looking into that situation, instead of in here answering a bunch of bureaucratic questions."

Marty Sanger looked flustered. "Miss Ray, you're obviously distraught."

"Oh, you think I'm distraught," she scoffed. "You're goddamn right I'm distraught. An operative lost his life, and you seem to be more interested in bringing up political bullshit! I can't help it that my Uncle is good friends with the President, any more than I can help it that both of my parents are dead at the hands of terrorists."

"Now you're being melodramatic," Thompson said, not phased in the least by her outburst. "And you're missing the point of what we're trying to do here."

"Which is what, exactly?"

"We are merely trying to get at the truth," Sanger offered. "You went to Afghanistan on a "reconnaissance mission" with a very seasoned operative. One who had Spec Ops experience behind him, yet you returned alive and well, and Mr. Brady is dead. So I can't help but wonder if the time you spent in captivity may have altered your views."

Kyra looked taken aback. "Are you trying to suggest I might somehow be responsible for Mike Brady's death, or that I'm in collusion?"

Thompson shrugged indifferently. "You claim nobody knew you were in country. So I have to ask, where the hell were you when the sniper put Brady in his crosshairs? How could an experienced sniper take out a seasoned operative with a clear headshot, yet a rookie, which is what you are, comes back with a few bruised ribs?"

Knowing Kyra was about to defend herself, and would not be diplomatic about it, Barry West sprung to his feet. "All right, that is enough, gentlemen! If you have any further questions regarding the capabilities of my operatives, I suggest you submit a memo and make an appointment with my office, or better yet, contact the President, who gave me the authority to put this team together and run it without interference. Otherwise, please excuse us, we have pressing work to get to."

The two of them stormed out of the office, before Thompson and Sanger had the chance to object.

CHAPTER 15

"Sorry sir, I spoke out of turn," Kyra said, as they marched down the corridor.

"And I suggest you don't make that mistake again." West said, peering at her out of the corner of his eye. "You know how the bureaucracy bullshit works in this town. I warned you they would try to bait you. That's the method they use when striving to get information, which doesn't necessarily mean they're looking for the truth, but data to prove the facts as they see them. Don't hold it against them; that's my job. Even though we're a black ops unit, we still have to deal with the fallout."

"Sir?" Kyra said while trying to keep up with his steady pace.

West held up his hand. "I already know what you're going to say."

"Then you know I need to see this through," she said. "With Tin and J.D.'s help, I can get to Hadley. You know he has information we can use. I don't want to pass the case off to other operatives. They don't have a stake in the outcome. He was Brady's asset—our asset. Let me see it through."

They arrived at the door to the Ops Center. West placed his hand on the biometric lock device, just to the right of the door. A green light appeared and the door slid open. Pausing, he glanced toward Kyra. "You don't think I'm going to let a couple of desk jockeys tell me how to run my agents?"

Kyra breathed a sigh of relief.

"I want to know about those weapons; where they were going, what the insurgents plan to do with them, and hopefully, stop them from wreaking any more havoc on our soldiers and innocent civilians."

Kyra nodded. "Hadley may not know where they were going, but I'm betting he can lead us to the individuals who do. I took the liberty of asking Tin and J.D. to check the GPS Brady planted."

West gave her a half smile. "You knew I'd give in"

Kyra shrugged. "I was counting on the fact that you wouldn't want our asset to be handed off to another team; black ops, or otherwise."

"You're goddamn right I don't," he said, as he loosened the tie around his shirt collar. "Now let's get busy. Dealing with suits always makes me feel like there is a noose around my neck."

He ushered her into the ops center and headed towards a desk that he set up as a temporary space to work with the team. West could no longer go out in the field because of his hearing loss issue, but he could aid in the preparation of the ops until they decided who would take Brady's place.

"Kyra, how'd it go?" J.D. said when they walked through the door. He was hovering over a table cluttered with gadgets. "Were you a good girl and give them the ole' yes sir, no sir routine expected of us?"

The team had a reputation for not dealing well with bureaucracy—whether it was from immaturity due to their youth, or the fact that their personalities were rebellious in nature—but that attitude had been tolerated, because they were able to thwart a few insurgent and Taliban attacks from information gleaned from their own personal assets. The powers that be were hoping their successes would continue, keeping with the notion that the safety of the troops and American citizens was more important than the hurt feelings of the suits in D.C.

Kyra shrugged as she walked over to join them. "You know me; I let my temper get the better of me, and couldn't keep my big mouth shut."

"No, really," Tin teased with sarcasm. "You have a temper?"

She gave him a mocking grin. "What's going on? With all the cool female gadgets, I feel like I've stepped onto the movie set of *Charlie's Angels*." She spotted a diamond encrusted watch and tried it on.

"Video camera?" she inquired.

Tin nodded, high on an overdose of espresso, he followed her around, showing her how things worked. "Let's say the operation calls for a fancy night on the town, you need to record it, but still look hot."

"Nice."

They paused to pay attention to a news alert playing on the big-screen monitor. The female news reporter said, "The White House confirmed today, that despite threats to interfere with the process, US Officials still plan to attend a meeting in Afghanistan to engage in talks regarding final troop movement, the election process, and the future of the region. Names of dignitaries planning to attend will not be released and the location of the meeting is being withheld..."

"Timely," West said, pondering what the news alert meant, and how it might affect his operatives.

"Withholding the location?" J.D. mocked, "How long before we see it splashed across internet news outlets?"

Tin picked up a remote. "Check this out," he said, grinning. As he worked the buttons, a tiny object that looked like a bumblebee flew off the table and fluttered around Kyra's face.

Kyra said, "What is it, a drone? It looks so real."

Tin smiled. "That's the idea." He dropped that remote, and picked up another. A hummingbird buzzed around the room, pausing in front of an old computer screen. Tin pushed a button on the remote. A sharp arrow disengaged like a bullet and shattered the screen with a violent punch.

"Is that strong enough to shatter bullet-proof glass?"

Tin maneuvered the bird over by a window, and was about to demonstrate, when Barry West cleared his throat. "A simple yes or no will do."

Tin shrugged. "In that case, no."

"Great," West said, "Now that we've all had some fun in toy town, can we dispense with the gadgetry business, and deal with the issue at hand. What did you find out about Thomas Hadley?"

Tin returned to his computer, pausing long enough to gulp down the rest of his canned espresso.

Kyra shook her head, and grinned. "You ever wonder why your ADD meds don't work?"

"Nope, I never do," he said, as his fingers raced over the keys. "Okay, so check this out." He loaded the tracking information onto his computer screen. A 3-D Google map showed up on the monitor. Tin pointed to a location on the screen. "So this is where the arms deal took place in the Sherpur District."

He traced his fingers along the map. "The tracking device shows Hadley leaving the meet then heading straight back to their hotel near Chicken Street— where Brady originally placed the tracking device on him. After a short time there, which I'm betting was long enough to pack his shit and check out, they headed to the airport to get out of dodge."

"So he's no longer in Afghanistan?" Kyra inquired, worried. "Then where did he go?"

Tin smiled. "He made a butt-load of cash for setting up the weapons deal, and he got paid for sharing it with us; a two-for-one deal."

J.D. clapped his hands together. "Hah, he's spending his hard-earned dough."

On the satellite map, Tin pointed to a dot designating Hadley's current location.

"Looks like we're going to the UAE," Kyra said, remembering the earlier report from Brady regarding Hadley's insatiable spending habits, Dubai being the closest thing to Las Vegas in the Middle East. "Any idea what hotel he's staying at?"

Tin grinned. "I can do you one better; I can tell you where he lives. He's making a decent living playing both sides, being an informant and setting up illegal deals. With the money he's made he bought an apartment building in Karama, Dubai. Keeps a two bedroom for himself and his bodyguard, or his current wife of the week, and then rents out the others. It's set up like a hotel; the building offers maid service, and they even have a concierge."

West rubbed his chin while he thought things through. "Okay, here's what we're gonna do," he said, after analyzing the information before him. He started grabbing items off his desk. "You three will head to the UAE as wealthy tourists on vacation. Tin will set up legends, provide the passports, and everything you need according to my specifications. To show we are trying to be team players, I'll clear everything with the SOOs. After I smooth things over, we'll discuss logistics and transportation, and then I'll put together a tactical op that'll give you enough room to maneuver on the fly, provided you pick up new Intel from Hadley. I'm going to put a call out to a buddy of mine; he's with the 380th

Air Expeditionary Wing, stationed at the Al Dhafra Air Base. You'll need weapons and gear, maybe even some modes of transportation while in country. He can help with that."

"Oh, hell yeah," J.D. said, jazzed to be going out in the field, and possibly get up in a chopper, again. He grabbed a duffel bag from under his computer, opened the safe at his desk, and was already preparing his gear.

West narrowed his eyes on Kyra. "I shouldn't have to remind you, but let's be clear; it's not just the assassin we're after here, you *will* stick to the op!"

Kyra slowly nodded her head in consent, but in the back of her mind she knew the assassin would wind up in her crosshairs, and she hoped it was some time soon.

As West headed toward the door, he turned back around, "Oh, and one more thing Kyra, you'll need to stop by and talk to the Doc before you go; you have to get cleared. No excuses. And I suggest if any of you have personal business that needs taken care of you might want to tend to it. You'll be leaving on a flight in the next twenty-four hours, and you should expect to be gone for an extended period of time."

With that, he was out the door, and Kyra was suddenly in a somber mood. "This one's for you, Brady," she said to herself.

CHAPTER 16

Arlington National Cemetery

The temperature was warm, the sun shining and the trees in full bloom, but that didn't help Kyra to overcome the sadness that started to consume her upon her arrival at Arlington National Cemetery. Walking past row after row of white marble headstones, she was reminded of a time when she was a young girl visiting the cemetery during a family vacation. It was Memorial weekend, she had just turned thirteen. Her parents demanded she go with them to honor military members who died serving this country.

She complained, whining as teens do, that it wasn't fair, that other girls her age were off enjoying picnics, swimming in the pool with their friends, or enjoying a day at the beach and meeting boys. Her father tried to explain the importance of Memorial Day, telling her that those great men and women died so that the rest of us could be free to do all the things that she wanted to do.

She listened and took it all in, but the significance of what he was saying didn't hit her, until later, when they were walking through the cemetery with flags waving at each headstone along the way for military members who died serving their country.

By the end of that Memorial weekend, she started to grasp the full meaning of patriotism, and it was a feeling that would deepen through the years.

The Victims of Terrorist Attack on the Pentagon is a memorial to honor victims of the September 11, 2001 attack on the Pentagon. Victims from the Pentagon and Flight 77 were buried as a group and the granite stone erected in their honor with the names of all the victims inscribed on the front.

Kyra arrived at the burial site and knelt down next to the memorial as her eyes perused the list of names, until she came to two that had diamonds to the left of them: Sergeant Terence 'Hotshot' Ray and Sharon Ray, her parents.

"Hi you two," she said, in an emotional voice. "Sorry I haven't been here in a while." As soon as she spoke the words, the tears began to fall.

General Jack Ray stood off in the distance, giving her a few moments of privacy walking up next to her. Before retiring from the army, Jack Ray was a four-star General with a commanding presence; well revered among the soldiers he commanded, as well as politicians across the hill, which carried over into his personal life and remained today.

His hair was dark with a touch of gray on the sides, and the grueling workout schedule he demanded of himself, kept him fit enough to compete with men half his age. Conservatively dressed in khaki pants, light blue shirt opened at the collar, and a navy-blue suit jacket, the man still had the presence of someone important—someone with connections and wielded power in the right places.

A distinguished career, he earned two Silver Stars for Valor, a Bronze Star, and three Distinguished Service Medals, knighted by Queen Elizabeth II, and honored with decorations from various countries. From the words of the current President of the United States: "General Jack Ray is one of the most respected Generals in my time."

"I thought I might find you here," he said softly, as he approached Kyra with his arms open for a paternal hug.

Kyra stood up and wiped the tears from her eyes as she walked into his embrace, letting his comfort wrap around her. To her, he was merely 'Uncle Ray'.

"I was sorry to hear about Mike," he said, with genuine warmth. "He served this country well, was a good friend, and hell of a patriot."

"After all the years he gave, now he's just another name on the wall, like so many others."

General Ray turned around and looked out at the thousands of monuments of those who gave for their country, keeping one arm draped around her shoulders. "None of us serve for the recognition, Kyra," he said, speaking from the heart. "It's something inside of us, an internal pull that guides us to want to look out for our fellow man. We don't do it for the glory."

They stood like that for several moments.

"Uncle Ray, there was nothing I could do."

He turned her around to face him, placed both hands on her shoulders and looked her square in the face. "Kyra Ray, don't you let those bureaucrats get under your skin! I know that's what this is about. They don't know what goes on out there in the field these days; it's a whole new ball game where the lines between good versus evil are often blurred. The suits in D.C. just sit behind their desks and draw conclusions based on their own opinions. Don't let that affect how you do your job."

"I'm trying not to, but I can't help but feel--"

"Guilty," he said, having suffered the same feeling several times through his career. "Hell girl, we all feel guilty when we lose someone that was standing out there next to us in the line of fire. There is a time to deal with those feelings. Right now you have to put it aside, use that military training and the skills you learned at The Farm; then follow the Intel and do what needs to be done. What'd your father always tell you?"

"Keep your head in the game, girl," Kyra said, as she envisioned her father sitting her down repeatedly through the years; during her sports competitions, when hunting and competing for the Thanksgiving dinner, and when climbing the Smokey Mountains during Christmas vacations to their log cabin in Gatlinburg, Tennessee. If he were alive when she went to boot camp and operative training, he would have been riding her then, too.

"That's right," Uncle Ray said. "Honor Brady by finishing what the two of you started. He was a smart man, Kyra. When he suggested doing a little recon in Afghanistan, it was because his instincts were telling him something bigger was going on. Somebody paid big money to take out two American agents."

Kyra glanced down at her feet, wondering if the information she was about to confess, should have been given to Barry West, her superior.

"Uncle Ray, the sniper let me live."

General Ray's head snapped around. "What are you saying, Kyra? Are you telling me the assassin had the opening for a shot, but didn't take it?"

"Uncle Ray, he had me dead to rights," she said, emphatically, still stunned by the whole ordeal. "He was as close as you and I. Put his gun to my forehead, finger on the trigger for the perfect headshot, then changed his mind after looking into my eyes."

He narrowed his eyes. "You left that out of the report."

"I left it out of the report," she confirmed. "You're the only one I've told."

General Ray took in a deep breath then let it out. "Then between us is where it will remain." He paused for a moment then hugged her close, and put his lips up to her ear, speaking almost conspiratorially, while he slipped a smartphone into her hand. "Kyra, once you get back out there in the field, if the shit gets too deep or your instincts are telling you not to trust a situation, reach out. I'll answer."

CHAPTER 17

The Gulfstream G650 taking the ATU team to the Dubai International Airport, had all the amenities of a working office with minor luxuries to feel the comforts of home.

After stowing his duffel bag, J.D. got comfortable in a leather recliner next to a window and settled in for a long flight while looking through a list of movies, and switching through the options.

Kyra and Tin sat in leather seats opposite each other, with a foldout desk in front of them. Tin had his laptop cranking, and a portable printer set up ready to go.

The three of them were dressed in casual attire; three rich twenty-something-year olds headed to the UAE to do a little sightseeing and shopping, check out the local beaches, and enjoy the festivities planned for the Formula 1 Grand Prix taking place on Yas Island.

"What is it?" Kyra said to Tin, when she noticed his eyes light up behind the computer screen. "Did you find something?"

He pulled himself away for a moment and spoke in an animated tone. "Think so. Well, maybe. I started by trying to track down financial institutions that our man Colton Cash Tate wires his money through. Boy, isn't that a mouthful, Colton Cash Tate. No wonder he calls himself Cash for short—even though I'm sure that's not the reason why."

"Tin, focus," Kyra said, waving her hands to get him back on track, mindful of the fact that what was once Brady's job now fell to her for the time being.

"Okay, so I found three accounts in Switzerland. Well, Zurich to be exact; where he also has a lavish home tucked up in the mountains, by the way. You know, in case you need to know that information, to pay the guy a visit." He flashed her with a smile as he printed the info and handed it to her.

Kyra tried to return the smile, even though she wasn't in the mood. No matter how impatient or focused everyone else was when prepping for the mission, Tin's infectious personality always seemed to shine through, even more when he was high on caffeine, which accounted for most of the time.

"Then I did a search for any large transactions out of each of those banks," he went on to say.

"What'd you find?"

Tin gave her an apologetic look. "Nada. Zip. Zilch. Zero. So, I decided to focus on smaller transactions."

"Tin, we're talking the professional hit of an operative, possibly two, seeing as I was a target too. The amount couldn't be small, could it?"

"You're assuming the assassin knew you were operatives," J.D. pointed out.

"And," Tin went on to say, holding up his finger to advise her that there was more. "How about a deposit wired to an account before the job. Then a payoff after the job was complete?"

"Please tell me you found one?"

"That I did," he said, smiling. Feeling very proud of himself, he rubbed his closed fist on his chest.

"Two days after Hadley contacted us to alert Brady to a possible arms deal, a large chunk of money was wired to a bank account in Zurich. Another payment to the same account the day after the hit. I'm betting that's our Hit man."

Kyra took a moment to digest the information; noting the fact that Brady was setting a surveillance op in motion right about the same time money was wired to take him out. Allegedly. "So, what was the asking price for the head of two operatives?"

Tin's expression turned serious, which was out of the norm. The discussion was a reminder that their friend was dead. "One million dollars," Tin said, in a subdued voice.

"We have a name for that account?"

"Still searching as we speak."

"How long do you think it'll take?"

"Could be a while," Tin said, with a shrug. "We're dealing with Switzerland; lots of red tape involved."

"Tin, we don't have time," she said, shooting him a look of irritation. Logically, she knew gathering Intel could be a slow process, but right now she was not good on patience.

J.D. caught her attitude, and became defensive. "Kyra, you may have been the one on the receiving end of a bullet, but Tin and I want the guy that killed Brady just as much as you do. Cut him some slack."

Kyra gave them both an apologetic look. "You're right, I'm sorry. I'm just not that good at the waiting game."

"None of us are," J.D. said.

"I'll keep up the pressure," Tin added with a smile, hoping to ease the tension.

J.D. turned toward Tin. "In the meantime, why don't you check the database, see if any swollen bank accounts turn up, in general."

"Already on it," Tin told him.

Kyra smiled. "Thanks for being patient with me, guys."

"We're a team," J.D. said, lying back to get a little shuteye. "That's what we do."

CHAPTER 18

Dubai International Airport
United Arab Emirates

After a twelve-hour flight, they arrived in Dubai in the early afternoon. Immigration was a breeze. Kyra had papers identifying her as an International model; J.D. her photographer, and Tin his assistant. They were on holiday, scoping out sights for a future photo shoot. With all the money they were flashing, the expensive luggage, and Kyra waltzing through the airport as only a professional model could, they weren't given a second glance—as far as the inspection went, anyway.

Before checking into the hotel, they decided to take a tour of the area and get the lay of the land. While J.D. collected the bags, Tin and Kyra rented a car.

The sun was blazing, and the view had Kyra mesmerized from the back seat. Tin was driving, J.D. was playing photographer. She remembered Brady calling it the Vegas of the Middle East. She had been to Vegas on many occasions; there were a few similarities. Both places were flashy, and full of glitz and glamour. Vegas had the Hoover Dam. On their current trip, they could see The Burj, the tallest skyscraper, gorgeous beaches, and the man-made islands were out of this world.

To keep up with the façade of being an International model and tourists on vacation, they rented the Junior Suite at the Sofitel Dubai Jumeirah Beach Hotel, which was more than adequate. The suite offered a living room area, with a mini kitchen and bar complete with a refrigerator. They opted for two queen sized beds, and a cot. The bathroom was contemporary with a luxurious tub and they had a view of the water.

They unloaded their suitcases, put their clothing in the drawers, and then locked the items they didn't want anyone to see inside the safe. While Tin checked the place for bugs, J.D. and Kyra discreetly did a quick recon with their binoculars.

Their room was on the twenty-fifth floor and facing the water, so there were minimal locations where someone could hide to spy on them, if they were discovered to be something other than tourists

"I think we're in the clear here," Kyra said.

J.D. nodded. "Only way to see into this room is via a helicopter or a telescopic lens on a boat out in the water."

"Bug free," Tin added.

J.D. walked over towards the desk, sat down in the chair and put his feet up, while he glanced at the brochure of the area. "There are five restaurants in this building, probably too expensive though since this is a 5-star hotel, but there's a whole shit-load of others in walking distance. They're all up and down the strand."

"Oh, so you're only here for the food," Kyra said, mockingly.

J.D. shrugged. "I'll take in the scenery, too," he said with a gleam in his eyes, "but this dude's got to eat something other than the peanuts and Scotch served on the plane."

Tin grabbed his laptop. "Kyra, when do you plan on surprising the asset?"

Kyra glanced at the clock on the nightstand. "J.D. has to hit the air base to collect all the necessary supplies. Why don't we pick up something to eat along the way, take a trip through Karama just to give me a feel for the area then head to the base after that? I'm thinking when the sun goes down would be a good time to pay a visit to Thomas Hadley."

J.D. jumped to his feet. "I'm all over that; let's do it."

CHAPTER 19

Karama, Dubai

A thirty-minute taxi ride from the hotel, Kyra ventured along the sidewalk near market center, fascinated by the stark difference between the streets lined with skyscrapers, five-star-hotels, and pristine beaches of Dubai, and the vendors offering Gucci and Dolce imitation handbags on the streets of Karama.

With her backpack slung over her shoulder, she tried to blend in with the tourists and locals haggling with the sales personnel trying to fill their shopping bags with the latest bargain, knowing that counterfeit goods were prevalent in the area. It was early evening, and the sun was finally slipping past beyond visibility.

She continued for several blocks then cut down a one-way street with rows of apartment buildings, hotels and cafés on both sides. After two blocks, she cut across the street and doubled back, observing her surroundings.

When she was sure no one was paying any attention to her, she walked into the lobby of the Karama Resort Apartments—the building owned by Thomas Hadley.

Palm trees stood on each side of the door, and in every corner of the main room. The walls were painted sky blue, with navy blue and gold Persian rugs on the floor. Two off-white sofas sat opposite a glass-top table, with oversized chairs at both ends.

Just to her right, an Asian man sat behind a desk with Concierge in gold letters on front. He hadn't noticed her yet, so she took the moment to look around. The elevators were just to her left. A young couple and a man in a suit were outside enjoying the patio, which was straight ahead through a set of French doors.

According to the research Tin did of the building, she had a half hour before two security guards arrived to take the night shift, and allowed the concierge to go home. She knew she was cutting it close, but she didn't want to come when it was still light out, and they couldn't wait until the following day.

With the decision made, she headed toward the elevators as if she knew where she was going. Inside, she donned a pair of leather gloves then hit the button for the fifth floor.

When the elevator door opened, she checked to make sure the hall was clear, and then headed for the stairway. Taking the steps two at a time, she exited on the seventh floor, looked left and then right.

Noticing a housekeeping cart with supplies sitting nearby, but seeing no maid, she walked over and pushed the cart over toward room 705. Grabbing a few clean towels from the center rack, she held them up to obstruct a view of her face, and then tapped on the door. "Housekeeping," she said, speaking with an accent.

When Thomas Hadley's bodyguard, Fuchs, opened the door, Kyra made a quick jab to the center of his throat, using her index and middle fingers, causing his pharynx to cave in, and preventing him from breathing.

Rendering him unconscious, she pushed her way through the door, and latched the lock behind her.

After dragging his body into the bathroom, she hefted it up over the side, and into the bathtub. She snatched a pair of flexi-cuffs and duct tape from her backpack, then secured his wrists and taped his ankles together, before covering his mouth.

After closing the bathroom door, she walked the perimeter of the living room, and removed any available weapons. Then she unlocked the sliding glass door, checking the exterior patio and balcony as she did. Once that was done, she took a seat in the corner chair, and waited for Hadley to arrive.

CHAPTER 20

It was over two hours before Kyra heard the card-key swipe through the magnetic device, then the apartment door swung open with a bang. Hadley and a female companion walked through the door. Inebriated, they nearly fell to the floor.

Kyra suppressed a laugh, when she heard the sounds of sloppy kissing, then a zipper coming undone.

The woman giggled. "Oh Hadley, I think somebody's excited."

"Let me get the light," Hadley uttered. "I can't find the damn buttons." He stumbled further into the room, and felt around the walls in search of the light switch.

The woman struggled to follow him, and tripped along the way, stumbling into a chair. "Oopsies," came her reply.

The light switched on then Hadley helped the woman to her feet, and they crash-landed on top of the sofa. They started to remove their clothing, and tossed it around the room.

Then Hadley suddenly spotted Kyra sitting in the chair in the corner of the room, and jolted upright, suddenly as sober as could be.

With a Sig Sauer P226 lying on her lap, and her backpack slung over her shoulder, she watched them as cool as a cucumber.

"Who the hell are you?" Hadley cried.

"Does Mike Brady ring a bell? He's dead, killed by a sniper at an arms deal set up by you."

Hadley's mouth opened wide, as his eyes darted around the room.

"Is this a bad time?" Kyra said, mildly amused by the near-naked couple.

Frustrated, Hadley hurried back into his clothes. The woman looked back and forth between Hadley and Kyra, confused. "Hadley?"

"Where's Fuchs?" Hadley said, suddenly concerned that his bodyguard was nowhere around.

"It's not him you need to worry about."

"Hadley, you didn't tell me someone else was joining us?" The woman said, slurring every other word.

Kyra rolled her eyes and stood up, holding her gun at her side. "Very well then, get rid of the bimbo."

The woman looked affronted. "Hey!"

Hadley was up on his feet, handing the woman her clothes and trying to usher her to the door.

"Why do I have to leave?" The woman squealed. "Tell her to leave!"

Hadley tried to help the woman dress. "Now is not a good time."

The woman noticed the gun and started to panic. "Hadley, why is she carrying a gun?"

Hadley opened the door and scooted her out, where she continued to squeal out in the hall.

Kyra slowly walked toward Hadley. "What'd you do with my bodyguard?"

"Your concern is touching." With the gun pointed at his head, she yanked him by his shirt and pulled him toward the bathroom. Opened it for Hadley to see Fuchs lying in the tub with his hands cuffed, his ankles bound, and a strip of tape over his mouth.

Awake now, Fuchs struggled and shot a menacing look toward Kyra.

"See, he's fine." She said, dismissing his reaction. She closed the bathroom door, and ushered Hadley back into the living room, pushing him down into a chair.

"Why can't you spies just leave me alone?" Hadley whined.

"Yeah, not going to happen; I need information."

"What information? I don't know anything."

Kyra gave him a look. "Think, long and hard."

His forehead started to perspire as he shook his head back and forth in denial. "What do you want from me?"

Kyra menacingly glanced at her weapon and aimed it toward Hadley for effect. "Two things, actually; I want you to tell me about Colton Cash Tate then give me the name of the man who purchased the weapons."

An immediate look of fear showed on his face, and his hands started to tremble. "I don't know what you're talking about."

"You're the one who told Brady about the deal."

He started to squirm. "Look, you got it all wrong."

"Save it Hadley." She walked over to his silver attaché case sitting on the coffee table, lifted up the stacks of cash and pulled out a transmitter. At the same time, she discreetly put a second transmitter in place then piled the cash on top.

"You've been tracking me?"

"We keep an eye on all deceitful informants. So stop wasting my time and spill it."

He got up and started to pace around the room, knowing he was busted. "The guy is a friggin' billionaire, okay. He's got businesses all over, owns real estate, stocks, he's the owner of a Formula 1 racing team, for cryin' out loud. All I did was broker the deal. I didn't supply the weapons."

"Yeah, well I don't give a shit," she shouted. "Those weapons are being used against American soldiers; my friends. Tell me who the buyer is."

Hadley's pacing became more frantic. "You think these people use their real identities?"

Kyra lost her patience. She made a quick move towards Hadley. "They're too arrogant not to. Either way, we know you sell out to anybody who's offering. Now give me the goddamn name." She pointed the gun at his crotch for emphasis. "Or, I'll save some lucky ladies from the pleasure of your goods. I lost a fellow operative out there!"

A noise came from out in the hall, then somebody pounded on the door. "Security Mr. Hadley, are you okay?"

Kyra put her fingers to her lips, advising him to keep quiet as she tapped the gun at his crotch.

Mr. Hadley? Open the door!" the security guard yelled.

Kyra grabbed the shirt at his neck, and moved the gun to his nose. "Give me the name!" She ordered, while glancing around the room.

"Tariq Jaffri, okay," Hadley yelled out.

"Now how do I get close to Colton Cash Tate?" At the same time, she pulled a rope out of her backpack with a large hook on one end.

Security pounded harder on the door. "Mr. Hadley, open up or I'm coming in!"

Hadley's eyes glanced toward the door. Kyra yanked him up by his shirt, and dragged him toward the sliding glass door.

"What about Cash?"

"He travels a lot, entertains on his yacht, The Sahara."

"Does his assassin travel with him?"

"I don't know anything about an assassin." Hadley whined, looking like he would do anything just to get rid of her.

The security guard suddenly crashed through the door. Kyra violently pushed Hadley toward him; they tumbled to the floor.

She bolted out onto the balcony. Hooking the rope to the top of the railing, she jumped over, slithered down several feet and dangled mid-air.

Kicked her feet off the wall, and then using the momentum, she jumped onto another balcony and crash-landed on the patio, just as Hadley and the guard came out the sliding glass door up above.

When the guard reached for his weapon, Kyra hit the window with the butt of her gun, shattering the glass. Placing her backpack over her head, she hurled herself through, and fell to the floor where a guitar player was serenading a group of girls.

"Whoa," he said, dazed and confused.

Kyra picked herself up off the floor and dusted the glass off her clothing. "Sorry 'bout the mess." She said, as she continued through the room and headed toward the front door. "You can send the bill to the owner of the building."

The sound of a bullet shattering the rest of the glass echoed in her ears from behind her as she ran down the hall and hit the stairs.

CHAPTER 21

Dressed in white shorts, an expensive polo shirt, and a pair of deck shoes with a cigar dangling from his lips, MI6 Agent, Logan Taylor sat comfortably on a motor boat anchored in the water near the Yas Marina. At first glance, he appeared to be a wealthy fisherman enjoying a vacation; his line was extended into the water and a box of bait sat nearby.

Hazel eyes looked around warily behind a pair of Ray Ban sunglasses, the earpiece in his ear and a monitor hidden from view, alerted Kyra to the fact that he was actually doing surveillance. She barreled past him on the seat of a Jet Ski, kicking up a wave of water and sending it raining down on him along the way.

"Bloody hell!" he yelled. Grabbing a towel, he stood up and was ready to yell again, until he realized who it was.

"I'll be dammed."

Kyra spun the Jet Ski back around and zoomed back toward the boat, easing the throttle to allow the Jet Ski to float alongside while she grabbed a hold of the rope tied to the eyehook.

"Sorry," she said, as she flipped her sunglasses up on her head to reveal the comical glint in her eyes, and gave him an engaging smile. "Did I get you wet?"

123

"Kyra Ray," he said, captivated by the sight of her. "I haven't seen you since ... when was it?"

"Over a year ago, in London," Kyra reminded him, "when your agency invited us to participate in a joint terrorist training exercise."

"Ah yes, the agency," he said, with regret. "We never did get to enjoy any personal time. Don't tell me we're working the same guy?"

Kyra glanced toward a two-hundred-fifty foot yacht moored along the pier, called The Sahara. "I don't know what you're talking about, Taylor. I'm here on vacation."

"Yeah, and I'm here for the camel races." Taylor teased. "So give it up. What's your Intel on this guy, Colton Cash Tate?"

She frowned. "You mean other than his penchant for arming terrorists?"

Taylor shook his head and with sarcasm, said, "You Americans are so cynical. What is it about a guy with a little money that always makes you suspicious?"

"Oh, I don't know," she added with her own dose of sarcasm. "Maybe it's the need to hide his money in Swiss bank accounts, yet have a handy hit man on standby. What's your excuse?"

"Just lots of chatter."

"Does that chatter include a meet and greet with a Pakistani by the name of Tariq Jaffri?" Kyra asked, and studied him to gauge his expression.

He didn't respond, but his facial expression belied the fact that he recognized the name.

"Thomas Hadley brokered a deal," Kyra said.

Taylor quipped, "Thomas Hadley, you say; must be hard up for cash, what with his fondness for gambling and spoiled members of the opposite sex that are into the *Fifty Shades of Grey* lifestyle. How does this guy Jaffri fall into it?"

Kyra shrugged, but her expression was serious. "He's putting weapons in the hands of the Taliban and insurgents in Afghanistan for starters."

Taylor masked his expression, which immediately gave Kyra the sense that he knew something, but wasn't sharing. She put the sunglasses back on the bridge of her nose, and glanced at the fishing line. "You might have better luck catching something if you put some bait on that line." She let go of the rope, and smiled then cranked the Jet Ski and sped off toward the harbor.

Taylor watched her until she disappeared from sight. He glanced toward the fishing line and then at the bait box, as if debating to do as she suggested.

"Nah," he said as he chuckled to himself then returned to his comfortable position.

CHAPTER 22

After discovering Cash docked The Sahara along the pier at the Yas Marina, the team had to find a secondary location to do surveillance. They opted to rent a cheap hotel room at the Park Inn, using J.D.'s false papers.

The room had two double beds, a small sofa, a club chair and a desk, where Tin was engrossed with information he was reading on his laptop. The kitchen area contained a small sink, with a microwave on the counter, and a small apartment-sized refrigerator underneath. Definitely not the 5-star they checked into upon their arrival.

J.D. had a camera sitting on a tri-pod, positioned behind the drapes near the sliding doors that opened out onto a balcony overlooking the harbor with the lens focused toward The Sahara.

"Logan Taylor is here?" J.D. said, surprised. "So how does he look?"

He rotated the camera lens over the Yachts, motorboats, and sailboats docked along the piers and moored in the water near the harbor. He noticed dozens of Jet Skis lined up along a floating pier, set up for a racing competition later in the day. The Tropicana Modeling Competition was also gearing up for the weekend, prepping for the Formula 1 Grand Prix festivities.

Summertime fun in the UAE, he mused.

Kyra entered the room barefoot, in a pair of tight jeans and a tank top, towel drying her hair from having just stepped out of the shower. She glanced at J.D. with a curious look on her face. "How's he look?"

Tin and J.D. glanced at each other and grinned.

"What?" J.D. mocked. "It's not like you don't know."

"Know what," she said, heading to the refrigerator to grab a bottle of water, and oblivious to what he was going on about.

J.D. shook his head. "C'mon, girl; you're telling me that when we flew to London and attended that joint terrorism exercise, you didn't pick up on the fact that the guy had a serious hard-on for you?"

"He does not," she said, gulping down half the bottle. "He's just a flirt, that's all."

"I'm a flirt," J.D. said.

Tin nodded. "You are."

"Logan Taylor on the other hand," J.D. continued, "is head-over-heels in lust with you."

Tin nodded. "He is."

Kyra shook her head. "You guys are nuts."

J.D. shrugged. "I'm tellin' ya, the guy's got it bad."

"Anyway," Kyra said, trying to ignore him. "Taylor was being tight lipped when I talked to him." She walked into the bathroom to hang up the wet towel

127

then returned combing out her hair. "I got the impression he knew something he wasn't sharing."

"You mean maybe something like this?" Tin said, motioning toward his laptop.

Kyra walked over behind him to have a look. On the screen was the photograph of Ahmed, the driver to Tariq Jaffri that she saw in Afghanistan. Next to the image was the title: British Agent, MI6.

"That bloody Brit held out on me," Kyra said.

J.D. said, "Nothing is ever as it seems."

"Deception, the name of the game," Tin added.

J.D. started to wave his hand in the air to get their attention. "Speaking of Taylor, we've got movement."

Kyra advanced toward the camera, peered through and said, "Well, that's one fine mess he's gotten himself into."

***

Needing a break, Taylor walked down to the lower deck to relieve himself and grabbed a bottle of Iced Tea out of the refrigerator on his way back up.

On his return, he slipped the tea into a cup holder then casually reached down for a pair of binoculars and peered through them. He perused the harbor, wishing he could get a look at Kyra, again, looking hot in that bikini. Catching no sight of her on the water, he looked out at the five-star hotels along the strip, the cluster of beaches, and the excitement starting to heat up on the water. The luxurious life of the UAE could definitely be addicting. Ah, but he was here to work.

He pivoted back around and moved the binoculars over the pier, until he settled on The Sahara, only to see Colton Cash Tate standing on the top deck staring back at him through his own set of binoculars.

Taylor pulled his eyes away and started toward the rope to pull up anchor. Before he could, The Chechen rose up out of the water, grabbed him by the arm and threw him into a floating hovercraft, and then rammed him on the head with the butt of a gun. Taylor went down; unconscious.

CHAPTER 23

Yas Marina Circuit was the location selected for the final race of the 2014 Formula 1 world championship. Unlike other races, Abu Dhabi takes place during the twilight hours with drivers racing into the night, switching from sunlight to spotlights.

Race cars wearing the insignias of their proud sponsors circled the track inside the stadium in a trial run performance in preparation for the upcoming Formula 1 Grand Prix. The owner of last year's winner, Colton Cash Tate, sat with a vivacious model on each arm in a private box-office seating while observing the action down below.

His driver, Donghai, stood behind them with his arms folded across his chest, his Asian eyes on sudden alert upon seeing LeClair saunter down the aisle in their direction.

Cash snapped his fingers in the air, and like a pair of obedient puppies, the models stood up on their Jimmy Choos, puckered their lips into a pout, and then sashayed up the aisle.

With a glint of amusement in his eyes, LeClair sent them a finger-wave goodbye, and then nonchalantly took a seat next to Cash.

"You're late," Cash pointed out, trying to assert his control over the meeting from the start.

LeClair gave him a dismissive shrug. "Am I?" There was no need to share that he had been there for quite some time, checking the security situation before approaching. He darted a quick sideways glance toward Donghai.

Cash didn't waste time on small talk; he cut right to the business at hand. He handed LeClair a pouch with the words: *For Your Eyes Only*, on front. "Someone whom I've had recent dealings with is talking to the wrong people. Find out whom."

LeClair shook his head as he looked inside the pouch. "Cell phones, internet, and you still feel the need to use cloak and dagger." Inside, he found the photographs of Thomas Hadley, Tariq Jaffri, and his driver, Ahmed.

Cash said, "One, or all of these men is an infiltrator."

LeClair raised his eyebrows. "Well, what would you have me do?"

Cash gave him a look that he recognized all too well.

"Jaffri is a Pakistani/American who currently resides in the United States," LeClair pointed out. "The same man you just got in bed with on a deal of weapons and drugs. Those weapons will wind up in the hands of terrorists, and the drugs sold to impede the minds of American children. Did you think he was a choir boy?"

Cash lifted the expensive cigar to his lips, took a hit and then let it out. "Is this task too difficult for you?" he said, with disdain. "Who are you to question me?"

LeClair let out a heavy sigh, knowing it was useless to continue. "It's been some time since I've been to the states."

"Am I not clear in my position as your master; do you not take orders from me?"

LeClair didn't rise to the bait. He studied the photos, contemplating what Cash wanted him to do, what the ramifications would be, and how difficult the task would be to see it through.

"Airport security may not be top rate, but it's improved considerably since September 11. Of course, if I were to go by water part of the way, my coastal contacts would expect their usual fee, and then there's the government or personal security of the targets."

"All I need to know is that you will take care of it," Cash said, impatient. "How you do so is irrelevant to me."

LeClair clenched his jaw; knowing the alternative was to wind up beaten and tortured like the last time he refused. On the other hand, a job of this magnitude would be quite a financial score, giving him the opportunity he was looking for, a chance to finally spring free. He gave Cash a self-assured look. "Everyone has their weakness."

Cash sat back, satisfied. "The usual fee, I presume?"

LeClair glanced toward the McClaren race car taking practice laps down on the track, wearing the logo of Cash Real Estate Developers in bold print on the car.

"Double," LeClair said, deadpan. "You're asking me to eliminate the issue with necessary travel to the states to take care of it. I'll need to lie low once the job's complete."

Cash scoffed. "The Chechen could do it for a pittance of that."

LeClair arrogantly shrugged then started to get up. "As you wish..."

Cash frowned. He knew LeClair was the better man equipped to handle this type of task, without drawing attention to Cash, himself. The Chechen was all brawn and no brain, and would lead investigators right back to them. He placed a hand on LeClair's shoulder advising him to stay.

"Greedy bastard."

LeClair's lips curved into a smile. "Same as before; half up front and the rest when the job's complete."

Cash paused for a moment. "Agreed. Come to my chalet after the job is complete then I will transfer final payoff."

The statement brought a glimmer of suspicion in LeClair's eyes. He studied Cash's face for a moment. "If I were you, I would also take a look into your own personal security."

Cash frowned. "My security is airtight; my people know better than to fuck around with me."

LeClair offered a cursory glance toward Donghai. "Naturally. Late night visits from men in black hoods tend to keep even the best of us conditioned."

Cash cocked his head to the side. "And I thought we'd gotten past all that. I take good care of my people; your bank account sure doesn't suffer. Make an appearance at the party, see for yourself how loyal my people are, and the amount of high society that stands right by my side."

"Loyalty," LeClair mused. "Now there's a word that's thrown around loosely." Then he disappeared up the aisle.

CHAPTER 24

Dressed as tourists in casual clothing, Kyra, J.D. and Tin, sat at an outdoor table at the *Stars N' Bars Sports Bar*, located at the Yas Marina. Enjoying an American meal of cheeseburgers and fries they laughed and joked, while taking photographs with a small Olympia digital camera, acting like all the other vacationers enjoying the festivities. What they were really doing was a little recon.

Cash was throwing a huge party on board The Sahara later that evening in celebration of the upcoming Formula 1 Grand Prix championship race scheduled the following week. Celebrities, politicians, wealthy business owners, the Formula 1 drivers and owners, and the models in the bikini competition would be attending.

Being as discreet as possible, J.D. and Tin were scoping out the area to check the security measures put in place for the party in an effort to provide a tactical plan to get Kyra on the boat. They thought about using her modelling background and just getting her an invitation, but nixed that idea. That meant she would have to be sociable with upper echelon and would have to do a little schmoozing, which was not one of her strong points under their current circumstances. While she had the looks of the international model, she had little desire to be a debutante. It was one thing to traipse through an airport allowing your photographer to carry your luggage, it was quite another to be put in a position to have to mingle with the celebrities and socialites.

Tin left his laptop in the safe at the hotel. Now, he was using his new *Samsung Galaxy Mega* to search the internet and using an app to formulate a plan to forward to their phones.

"Okay, here's what I've observed so far," J.D. said, in between bites of his food. "The Sahara is moored at the northern end of the pier and overlooks the marina circuit. There are four levels above water, two below. A red carpet entrance is set up at the plank, where limousines, Sedans, sports cars, and buses drop off guests to the party which will be held on the main deck."

"So we're talking lavish affair," Kyra said, following up with a groan.

J.D. smiled and jokingly said, "I'm sure if you arrived topless, jeans would probably be acceptable."

Kyra smirked. "Cute."

Tin looked around then whispered. "Not much in the way of security on the top deck; I assume that is so they don't draw too much attention."

Kyra nodded. "If the authorities in the UAE learned of Cash's illegal arms deals with terrorists, he'd be booted out of the country, even if his race car was last year's winner of the Formula 1 Grand Prix."

"Exactly," Tin said. "Okay, so at 2100 hours the party should be in full swing, and everyone's attention should be on the circuit, where the new Ferrari and the McClaren will do a test exhibition around the track."

J.D. added. "Armed guards—dressed in white pants, white shirts, and blue jackets—man the entrances, and stand guard at both ends. They also alternate walking the perimeter of the boat in half-hour intervals. So we've got a small window of time to get you on board."

Tin nodded. "I also noticed a Hovercraft at the south end of the boat, but again with the guards disguised."

Kyra glanced over at J.D. "Did you set up everything we would need with West's friends at the base?"

"Affirmative," he said. "I also called your Uncle Ray like you suggested. He put me in touch with a former Navy SEAL who is here in the UAE helping with training at the Zayed Military City. Your Uncle informed him that we were here on the hush, hush, but he said he could help us get what we need. We should be all set. Between the guests attending the party, and those that will be hanging out on small boats and jet skis in the water, we could pass without notice. Cash will want his private security to keep a low profile, so once you're off the boat, the escape plan should be easier."

"Nothing is ever easy," Kyra said, as she relaxed in her seat and took in the scenery through the eyes of a tourist. "This place really is magnificent. I've never seen anything like it. You've got the beaches, a place to dock your boat—whether it's a small speed boat or a mega yacht—restaurants for both the wealthy and the middle-class family, the race track, and the water park for kids and parents alike, and all in one location."

Tin and J.D. roared with laughter.

"What?"

"You're like a walking brochure for a travel agency for the UAE," J.D. said.

Kyra turned serious. "Yeah, and it just goes to show you that even amongst all this beauty, there are dangerous people lurking in the shadows who intend to cause harm and chaos if they don't get what they want."

CHAPTER 25

On the lower deck of the yacht, Logan Taylor sat handcuffed to a wood chair in a room cluttered with cargos and crates. His face and upper body looked like he went a few rounds in the boxing ring; swollen and bruised with cuts down his lip and splatters of blood on his shirt and crates behind him. His chin was slumped down toward his chest, his eyes closed to avoid the bright light of the spotlight directed toward him.

Dressed in dark fatigues, The Chechen smacked his fist in his palm, prepping for another round. "Are you ready to confess who hired you?"

Taylor slowly lifted his head up and peered at him through his left eye; his right one was swollen shut. Even in his current predicament, he still appeared cool and collected.

"All right, all right, I'll tell you," Taylor said, spitting blood out as he spoke.

The Chechen gave him a smile of satisfaction, and waited for the confession.

"I'm a private dick hired by your wife," Taylor stuttered, then tried to appear sympathetic. "She says you've been having trouble satisfying her, figured there must be a reason."

"You stupid Brit!" The Chechen roared, as he punched him across the face in response.

"No need to be so defensive, mate," Taylor mocked, adjusting his jaw and knowing he'd be slammed again, but not giving a damn. "It's a common problem among men these days. That's why the pharmaceutical companies are making so much dough on Viagra and Cialis. Not that I have that problem myself, but I hear they work wonders."

The Chechen delivered another blow, causing Taylor to cough up more blood.

"Listen chap, would you mind keeping the shots below the face? The women tell me they kind of like the one I have."

A shadow appeared on the wall behind them as LeClair cautiously stepped into the room, but remained out of Taylor's sight. His demeanor changed at the sight of a man being cuffed and beaten by The Chechen; bringing back dark memories of the times when he was on the receiving end of a similar fate.

"What are you doing down here?" The Chechen said, irritated by the interruption. "I'm conducting business."

LeClair shrugged, trying to appear indifferent while studying the injuries of the man in the chair. "Yes, I can see that, though I'm confused as to how you think you're being productive."

"He's not giving me answers," The Chechen said. "I'm trying to convince him...doesn't concern you."

Taylor tried to twist his head around to get a glimpse of the man in the shadows, but couldn't see his face. He turned back toward The Chechen, and said in a glib tone. "I knew you were just a puppet being pulled by strings, you're too dim to handle this shit on your own."

The Chechen delivered three quick punches to the gut—right, left, right—and then another angry blow to the face. The force was so powerful; Taylor and the chair went flying.

"Enough!" LeClair barked, feeling the rage building up inside of him as if he was actually the one in the chair. "Pummeling him to death is not going to compel him to answer you."

The Chechen glanced toward LeClair with a sneer, knowing months of beatings worked on him. "You're evidence to the contrary, but since when do you give the orders?"

"Help the man up!" LeClair ordered, disregarding his question and speaking in an authoritative tone.

The Chechen grudgingly pulled the chair back up, and adjusted the rope binding Taylor.

"I'm sorry," LeClair went on to say, "You'll have to excuse him. I'm afraid he's not very diplomatic in his approach."

Taylor let out a half-hearted laugh. "Terrorists and diplomacy in the same sentence, who'd a thought."

"Leave him," LeClair ordered, "you're needed upstairs."

141

The Chechen didn't know whether or not to believe him, but it was better to air on the side of caution. He turned back toward Taylor, and offered him a predatory glare. "I'll be back to finish this, soon!"

Taylor tried to maintain his sense of humor, and give the dim man a smile, but his lips wouldn't cooperate. "Bring some popcorn," he stuttered as he spit out blood. "I like watching B-rated boxing matches."

The Chechen sneered. "I'll give you the choice of which bone I rip off first."

Taylor couldn't help himself; he shivered at the sound of that.

CHAPTER 26

Tiny specks that looked like diamonds lit up the midnight sky as the white-gloved-waves rocked the luxurious yachts owned by wealthy individuals from all over the world, and floating in the turquoise water at the marina. Flying high above the yachts in a black flight suit, Kyra parachuted toward The Sahara, scoping out the security through a pair of night vision goggles (NVG's).

As Tin and J.D. verified earlier, all was clear.

A hovercraft sat at the south end of the yacht, with four armed guards on board posing as security for the party, with their eyes focused on the track. Guards in blue jackets, armed with two-way radios—guns were probably under the jackets—walked the perimeter of all four decks above water, doing so in thirty-minute intervals.

Hoots and hollers echoed from the first floor of the yacht, with partiers watching the competition between two Formula 1 drivers vying for the lead spot on the track during one night of fun.

"Uh oh, you've got company," Tin said into her earpiece, "single guard just to the left of the swimming pool, lighting up a cigarette."

"I see him," Kyra said. "It was too late to change the plan, so she stowed the goggles and prepared herself for a landing. Legs out, knees bent, hips loose, and then whoop—she slammed down into the guard, taking him down to the ground and knocking him unconscious.

Moving the gear out of the way, she did a quick search of him and discarded the Glock holstered on his shoulder under one of the lounge chair cushions.

She began to unzip the flight suit, revealing a sequined mini-dress barely covering a pair of long-tanned legs. She removed the helmet to let her long hair fall free then turned around to face a second guard walking around the perimeter at that precise time.

"What the..." the guard said, totally flummoxed by the woman in front him, and not yet seeing the other guard flat on the ground.

Kyra gave him an innocent smile, as she walked toward him with her hips swaying. "Are you here for my invitation?"

The guard was stunned for a moment, unsure of the situation since she looked like one of the models. Before he realized it, she was right in front of him delivering a fisted palm to the nose, and a knee to the crotch.

"That'll teach you not to sneak up on a lady," she said, not even winded.

Stunned, the guard doubled over, so she followed it with a scissor kick that knocked his head back onto a glass-top table—he was out cold.

With both guards down, she pulled a rope out of the bag attached to her harness, and quickly tied the two together. Then she grabbed a roll of duct tape, and secured their mouths from yelling out.

***

The MH-6M Little Bird helicopter that J.D. was borrowing sat in the middle of a field in Zayed Military City, not too far away from the marina. In the pilot seat, J.D. flipped through a *Victoria Secret* catalogue, glancing through the lingerie selection for summer.

In the back of the chopper Tin sat across from a Samsonite case equipped with high-tech surveillance equipment. As he prepped the CCTV monitor, he glanced over at J.D. with an amused look. "Does your girlfriend know about your fetish for women's lingerie?"

J.D. smiled at the joke, since everyone knew it was the models he was checking out. "She's got no problem with it," he said, returning the sarcasm, "just as long as I share."

"Is that part of the whole "relationship" thing?"

"Tin, you do know being in a relationship is not a thing?"

Tin shrugged indifferently. "So how does it work, exactly? I mean, say you're out at a bar, you meet a woman you like--"

J.D. gave Tin a strange look. "No different than when you meet a woman. You say hello, offer to buy them a drink."

"Yeah, I know, but it's not like you can take 'em back to your house for dinner and a little fun. You live with your parents."

Tin glanced over at J.D., an odd realization dawning on him. "You don't right? I mean, that would be weird, to have your mom and dad in the house with some hot chick you want to have a late-night romp with, or whatever you're calling it these days. Can't even imagine ... you really need to get your own place, dude."

J.D. shook his head. "Who needs their own place when there's always somebody around to do the laundry, and cook some awesome homemade meals? Why would I give all that up, when the chicks will just push me into marriage? Living at home, I can take my time and evaluate the prospects. Besides, haven't you ever heard of a hotel, you jack-wad?"

"Jack-wad?" Tin said with a laugh. "Is that even a word?"

CHAPTER 27

With both guards secured, Kyra whipped out her weapon, the Sig Sauer P226, a KA-BAR, and other miscellaneous equipment from her duffel bag. She strapped the gun to the holster on her left leg and the blade on her right. She verified the contents of a small handbag: a canister, tube of lipstick, lock picks and another contraption; then she placed an eraser-size earpiece in her ear. She grabbed the rope gear from the duffel before she hid the bag under the cover of a Jet Ski that sat on the end of the yacht.

"Ready, sports fans?" Kyra said, as she tapped on a small silver broche, which was really a camera pinned to her dress. "Got a visual?

***

J.D. tossed the catalogue off to the side, and joined Tin at the equipment.

Tin turned his baseball cap around and got into game mode. He focused his attention on the monitor, which was now displaying the images that Kyra was seeing through the camera.

"Any other trouble?" Tin said.

"Only those minor annoyances."

147

J.D. chimed in, "Still on the top deck I see."

"Not for long," she said.

The railing along each floor was waist high with bars about three to four inches in diameter. She quickly secured a rope to the top one, slipped her long legs over the railing and then dropped down the side. At the sound of guards approaching on each floor, she paused and dangled in the air until they passed, and then continued.

She dropped in on three middle-aged women gathered for a smoke and gossip session on the main deck. "Don't mind me ladies," she said. "I just hate making a boring entrance to these things."

The women glanced at the rope dangling in the air, and then looked at Kyra, stunned to see her merely adjust her dress and confidently stroll toward the party.

A few feet away, Dalton LeClair stepped onto the main deck, stepping up from one of the floors down below. He spotted Kyra as she dropped in on the women. Realizing immediately, that she was the woman from Afghanistan, he remained in the shadows and watched her, mesmerized and intrigued. The last time he saw her he was wearing a mask, but they were so close, she might have seen his eyes.

"Who is she?" he heard one of the women say.

The other women shook their heads, looking perplexed. Then, a worried frown suddenly burrowed their foreheads.

One of the other women said, "I think I'll just go check on my husband."

LeClair smiled, when the others hurried after her to do the same. "Smart move, ladies," he said to himself.

Once they left the area, he stepped out of the shadows then felt an overwhelming urge to follow her, and headed toward the party.

What was she doing here?

A small-piece orchestra played soft music from a stage in the corner when Kyra slipped into the large salon serving as the reception area for the party. She could hear a popular band playing further down the main deck, where the party would wind up as the evening progressed and the drinking continued.

To her left, she spotted a circular mahogany bar with stools all the way around, and two bartenders in white uniforms tending to the guests. Large flat-screen TVs hung on the wall behind it, showing snippets of the previous years' Formula 1 races, which kept the conversation flowing.

She meandered through all the beautiful people. Straight ahead, four white sofas squared off around a large glass table in the center; navy blue and red pillows matched the Persian rugs of red, navy-blue, and gold underneath. Kyra couldn't help but notice that the yacht, its design, and the added luxurious décor, were all a means of showing stature for Colton Cash Tate.

Speaking of Cash, she spotted him at the far end of the room. A young model-type was on each arm as he

149

mingled with individuals she assumed were dignitaries and politicians; a few of them wore the traditional robe, while others wore conservative suits. His driver, Donghai remained close to his side, but The Chechen was nowhere around.

Kyra didn't think they would recognize her, since she never got close to them in Afghanistan. Even if he did order the hit, how would he have known what she looked like? As far as anyone at the party knew, she was just another wannabe here to enjoy the party, see whom she could meet, and get invites to other posh parties.

"Do we know where Taylor is?" Kyra mumbled into her microphone.

"According to the blueprint, there is a storage room two floors down," Tin said.

"Oh, and Kyra... be careful," J.D. added.

"Am I ever anything but?"

"Well, there was the time you marched into a gangbangers' club all by yourself, hoping to stop the initiation ceremony going on inside."

"They weren't gangbangers; it was a biker club ... and bikers get a bad rep."

Tin added, "And what about the time you jumped out of a private airplane without a parachute."

"Really; you're using that one ... the plane was only a dozen or so feet above the Pacific Ocean in the middle of summer. Okay, okay, I'll be careful."

"That's all we ask," J. D. said.

Kyra worked the room with poised confidence, keeping a smile on her face and looking around, but not at anyone in particular. As a new arrival, some of them stopped to stare. She paused in the middle of the room and reached into the handbag for a tube of lipstick, and then seductively brushed it over her lips. Unknown to the guests the tube photographed their smiles as she scanned the crowd.

LeClair slipped into the room, but remained at the back of the bar and out of her eyesight. There was something about her and he couldn't help himself, he was drawn to her. He watched as a suave, twenty-something man in an Armani suit made his way through the crowd, and zeroed in on her.

Mr. Armani approached her and boldly placed his hand on her arm. "Looks like you and I are both without dates," he said to her, beaming with confidence. "How about we show up these stuffed shirts, and brighten up the dance floor?"

Kyra barely gave him a glance, and instead locked eyes on the hand placed on her arm, convincing him to remove it. "Sorry, I don't do Armani," she said, and she walked away without giving him another thought.

Laughter echoed in her ear. "Love that girl!" J.D. said.

LeClair smiled at the confident nature in which she handled herself. His eyes continued to follow her, until she disappeared from the room, and then he realized where she was going.

CHAPTER 28

Kyra walked two hundred feet down the corridor, trying to stay quiet to get a lead on the guard at the end. He had his back to her, just a few more feet away. They were probably the same height with her three-inch heels, considering she had a five-foot-ten frame.

She tiptoed forward, came up behind him then wrapped an arm around his neck and applied just enough pressure to make him pass out. She moved him out of view, just as another guard stepped around the corner.

"Stop right there!" the guard ordered, speaking with a thick accent as he jammed his gun into her right side.

Kyra paused for a brief moment then quickly pulled the arm holding the gun forward then karate chopped it, causing him to lose the feeling in his arm and drop the gun to the ground. Then she lowered her upper body, and swung her left elbow back and whacked him in the nose. Blood sprayed from the impact.

As he moaned and reached for his face, she followed it up with a sidekick that sent him falling backwards, bashing his head into the railing and rendering him unconscious. She positioned him next to the other downed guard.

She did a quick double-check for any others then hurried down the spiral staircase, and onto the lower level. At the same time, The Chechen stepped out of the maintenance room wiping blood from his hands.

Their eyes locked, and both immediately made moves toward their weapons. Kyra dropped and rolled out of the way of a bullet meant for her head, and let loose with the KA-BAR. It landed dead center to The Chechen's chest. Stunned and unsteady on his feet, Kyra rushed toward him and followed it up with a swift kick that sent him crashing to the ground.

She knew he wouldn't be down long. She did another quick check of the area, and then opened the door to the supply room and braced herself for what she might see.

"Better wrap this up, Kyra," Tin chimed in the through her earpiece. "Got us a curious hostile on the roof."

Kyra dragged The Chechen inside the storage room. "Working fast as I can here, boys."

"Hey, I'm just the messenger," Tin added, amused.

"Isn't it customary for the guy to rescue the girl?" Logan Taylor mumbled from behind her.

"Considering what century this is, I'd say that cliché is highly overrated," Kyra said as she swiveled around to see him seated in a chair, and beaten to a bloody pulp.

"Sheesh, that is one ugly mug," she said, horrified by the injuries, but trying to maintain the sarcastic humor.

"Yeah, I told him the gals like the way I looked, but he didn't feel the need to listen."

"This is one fine mess you've gotten yourself into, Taylor. Can you move?"

Taylor chuckled. "I'll manage. You don't think I'm going to stick around here?"

"Britain's glory boy is alive," she said into the mic.

"Then get him the hell out, and let's blow this private shindig," Tin said.

"They damage his face?" J.D. said, trying to throw in some levity.

"Damn J.D.," Tin joked. "Now is not the time to be worrying about your competition."

Kyra shook her head at the chatter from the radio. "Play nice boys."

Taylor looked at the blade in The Chechen's chest. "Bullocks, I wanted to do that. You save any for me?"

Kyra retrieved the lock picks and proceeded to unlock the cuffs, and untie the rope securing him to the chair. "There's plenty more outside."

Once he was free, he rubbed his wrists and checked his ribs to see if they were broken.

Kyra pulled out her Sig Sauer and tossed it to him. "Use it wisely," she told him.

Taylor said, "Now that I'm free, I don't intend to muck it up."

Before exiting the room, Taylor violently pulled the blade out of The Chechen's chest. "Might have need of that, mate."

154

They opened the door a crack and checked for guards. When they assumed it was all clear, they slipped out of the supply room and closed the door behind them.

Kyra spoke into the mic. "Okay boys, saddle up. We're headed out."

"None too soon for me," J.D. said, and the noise from the helicopter echoed through the earpiece.

CHAPTER 29

Kyra and Taylor made their way back through the corridor, keeping their eyes and ears peeled. They paused at the sound of boots headed their way.

"Somebody is on the move," Taylor whispered, "coming fast up the stairs behind us."

"Darn, thought we'd have a little time before word went out."

Kyra pulled out a retractable crossbow and clicked it open. Leaning out over the exterior railing, she shot it up to the top deck of the yacht, yanking on it until the rope locked and was secure.

"Go, go, go," she ordered Taylor, pushing him toward the rope.

Taylor climbed up onto the railing, and then using the rope, proceeded to pull his body up to the roof.

Kyra reached inside her handbag, and pulled out a Flash Bang Grenade. When the guards cleared the steps and headed their way, she pulled the ring on the FBG and tossed it to the floor ahead of them. A big BOOM sounded; pushing two guards back from fear then a huge cloud of smoke filtered the air, giving them zero visibility.

156

Kyra took that moment to latch onto the rope, and hauled herself up, moving in acrobat-like prowess up the side of the boat.

"Nice work," Taylor said, helping her over the railing on the roof.

Seeing the smoke clearing, he leaned over and fired two shots from the Sig Sauer, then followed Kyra to the far end of the roof where she grabbed her bag from under the Jet Ski cover.

"Saw an IRB when they brought me on here earlier," Taylor shouted.

"Forget that!" Kyra shouted back, and pointed toward a group of Jet Skis docked at a floating pier. "There's a Kawasaki STX-R in that mix; it'll start by pulling the ignition switch."

She tossed the duffel bag to Taylor. "There are more guns and ammo in there."

Taylor glanced down and mentally measured the distance between the rooftop of the yacht, and the water down below. "You want me to jump?"

Kyra said, "Feel free to stick around if you want."

A bullet ricochet off an antenna inches away from him, making him duck and turn to see a guard just coming up the steps from down below.

Taylor whipped the KA-BAR at the guard and struck him in the leg, and then followed it up with a round of bullets. "On second thought; I sure hope this duffel bag is waterproof!"

He tossed the gun inside, zipped it back up. Simultaneously, the two of them slipped their legs over the railing, glanced at each other, and jumped down into the tropical water. When they came back up to the surface, they swam toward the pier.

Taylor threw the duffel up onto the pier, and then pushed himself up then lowered his hand down to Kyra.

Bullets ripped into the fiberglass material around them from a pair of silenced pistols. They looked back to see two guards standing on the yacht opening fire, right before The Chechen showed up to stop them; they didn't want to draw the attention of authorities.

"Looks like the insane giant is up and around," Taylor said. He opened the duffel and retrieved the gun while they moved toward the Jet Ski.

While Kyra opened the front trunk and disassembled the ignition switch, he kept watch. There was an immediate lull in the excitement almost as if the guards were called off.

Kyra hopped on the Kawasaki, pulled the choke and hit the green power button on the left handle. The motor purred to life as she rotated the throttle. Taylor untied the rope securing it to the dock.

"Can't hold it in place much longer. Let's go!"

Taylor jumped onto the back, and she cranked the throttle giving it gas.

"Oh shit!" Taylor yelled, as the Jet Ski surged through the water. Taylor grabbed onto Kyra and held tight. "I gather you've had a lot of experience on these?"

"It's just a dirt bike on water," Kyra shouted in return.

They powered through the Marina, just like all the other Jet Skis there enjoying the fun, giving them the false sense of security that they were in the clear.

Taylor yelled out in relief. "Damn fine job, Kyra."

A silenced bullet shattered their joy, when it ripped a hole in the side of the Jet Ski. Others peppered the water all around them. They turned around to see a hovercraft with four armed men was hot on their trail.

Kyra shouted, "No time to gloat. Do what you do best."

"On it," Taylor said. He reached into the duffel, pulled out the H&K USP Compact and checked the ammo then whipped around. He aimed the gun at the man in control of the hovercraft and fired several rounds. The speed and constant movement prevented him from making contact.

Kyra maneuvered the Jet Ski back and forth to avoid being a target. She yelled, "Could use a little help here!"

Taylor fired several more rounds, hitting one of the guards who fell into the water from the blast, but still failed to get the driver.

"I thought you were an excellent shot?"

The hovercraft was closing in on them with the guards continuously firing.

"Yeah, when I'm standing still," Taylor responded.

"So shoot at the skirt!"

"Bearing down on you now," J.D. shouted into the Kyra's earpiece. Kyra looked up to see the helicopter off in the distance with the ladder lowered.

One of the guards on the hovercraft tried to jump toward Taylor. Kyra swerved to the right to get out of his path, and he plunged into the water.

Kyra noticed a ski-ramp in their path. "Hold on," she yelled to Taylor.

Taylor chanced a look. "You couldn't have avoided it?"

"I've been too busy dodging bullets!"

Taylor grabbed tighter to her waist, as the Jet Ski soared up the ramp then flew through the air and slammed into the rocky waters once again.

The helicopter finally circled overhead, with the ladder hanging above their heads.

"Get yourself up, I'll hold 'em off," Taylor ordered.

"Like you've been doing all along?"

"I'm feeling a little unappreciated here!"

He turned and fired several rounds at the hovercraft, while Kyra attempted to balance her feet on the Jet Ski. She jumped for the ladder, grabbed hold and climbed up. Midway, she locked her leg on the ladder like a circus acrobat and lowered her upper body down to extend her hand.

"Get your ass up here!"

Taylor proffered another round of bullets at the hovercraft, this time striking several holes in the skirt, the driver finally lost control of the craft.

Taylor balanced his feet like a surfer, and reached up for Kyra. She grabbed hold of his arms and hoisted him up right before the hovercraft rammed into the Jet Ski. They dangled on the ladder as the two remaining guards continued to fire their weapons.

The helicopter altered its course and moved out of the path. A bullet ricocheted off one of the rotors, making the chopper shake. Kyra and Taylor were hanging on for dear life.

They watched the Jet Ski and hovercraft suddenly veer off course, headed inland. The guards jumped into the water, seconds before the vehicles crashed into the side of another pier.

"That was one helluva ride!' Taylor yelled, after they were in the clear. "I guess I owe you a debt of gratitude."

Kyra gave him a serious glare. "I suggest you start, by telling me the truth about the MI6 agent you have working with Tariq Jaffri."

***

Back on the yacht, LeClair stood on the main deck looking through a set of NVG's, watching Kyra and Taylor make their escape, and with a smile on his face.

161

CHAPTER 30

Prepping for an operation in another country can be tricky, and you need the ability to switch gears on the fly. The original plan was to get more Intel from the asset. Making the decision to rescue Taylor meant they would be putting lives in jeopardy; not just theirs, but the innocent people at the party. Anything could have happened.

They were counting on the fact that Cash would want to keep his illegal enterprises quiet, and therefore, wouldn't order an all-out surge by his security forces through the marina. What little did go down, would no doubt be settled with a few polite payments from Cash, and an apology to the UAE that someone had a few too many drinks at the party, and behavior got a little out of hand. By the time authorities discovered the facts Kyra and her team would either have more evidence against Colton Cash Tate, or would already be out of the country.

J.D. returned the helicopter to the training center at Zayed Military City where former American military members were in country training UAE forces. When Uncle Ray informed them that we were prepping for a mission—no explanation needed—they offered use of the helicopter and supplied them with the Flash Bang

Grenade and Crossbow. Barry West's friend at the air base supplied the guns and KA-Bars; he said it was wise to have connections and friends across the country.

They returned to the Park Inn Hotel and cleared everything out then borrowed cots for the night at Taylor's field office after he got a medical check-up. The MI6 had connections in Abu Dhabi where some were intelligence members in the UAE.

Tin was back to work on his laptop, taking images from the lipstick camera, and running them against the database.

The following morning, Taylor gave Kyra a tour of the industrial warehouse housing a small contingent of agents, who stood to shake her hand and thank her for saving Taylor—even though some of them joked that they would have left him there.

"You're right," Taylor said, after a round of introductions. "I do owe you an apology for not telling you about Ahmed, especially now that you've gone and saved my life." He glanced at her and winked, using the eye that wasn't quite as swollen.

"Make me regret it, I'll kill you myself," Kyra said, By her stoned-face expression, he got the impression she meant it.

"So how long has he been undercover with Tariq Jaffri?"

"Little over six months," Taylor said. He stopped at a coffee machine, poured himself a cup and dropped in the same amount of sugar. When he offered a cup to

Kyra, she declined. "Three of those months, he was under as Jaffri's personal driver."

Kyra walked over to a vending machine, put some money in, and hit the button for a bottle of water.

"Cash let the right people know he had a continuous flow of weapons and drugs. Hadley, seeing the dollar signs, took the bait. He put the word out to the terrorist community. Jaffri responded. According to Ahmed, he purchased a truckload of weapons, which are in transit; expects to take delivery of a shipment of drugs somewhere in the states."

Kyra took several gulps of water. "But, you're saying the weapons are not going to make it into the hands of insurgents?'

Taylor gave her an overly confident smile, and led her into the communications room. "The ICRC truck left the Sherpur District and is currently making its way through the mountains of Afghanistan expected to make delivery to the Taliban and insurgents. Unfortunately for them, we have our own brand of insurgents ready to intercede."

The room went dark, save for the large CCTV Monitors showing satellite images. Uniformed officers and MI6 agents operated the computers; real-time images appeared on the screen: The ICRC truck filled with the weapons travelled over a dirt road with mud walls covered in grape vines along the way. With no US posts on those particular dirt tracks, no drones or surveillance helicopters were expected to fly overhead.

After a few more miles, the truck turned onto another dirt road. Minutes passed then two bullet-ridden Toyota pick-ups came out of nowhere and pulled in front of the truck, forcing it to stop then two more blocked it from the rear. Dark-skinned men in scarves and traditional Afghani attire and armed with AK-47s—looking like members of the Taliban or Afghani Warlords—jumped out of the Toyotas and surrounded the ICRC truck.

"Get out of the truck with your hands where we can see them," one of the men yelled in Pashto.

With the AK-47s directed at their faces, the men complied; assuming it was the Taliban and insurgents they were coming to see.

"Face down in the dirt with your belly flat on the ground," the Pashto speaking man continued.

Once Cash's men were down, one of the scarfed men pulled their hands down behind their back then zip-tied their wrists. Another climbed up into the driver's seat of the ICRC truck, and then the others hopped back into the Toyotas. With some quick maneuvering on the dirt road, the Toyotas escorted the truck out of the area. Cash's men remained cuffed on the side of the road.

"Leaving Cash's men alive on the side of the road has a purpose?" Kyra asked Taylor once the takedown was completed.

He walked over to the wall and flipped the light switch. When he returned, she thought he was grinning, but couldn't tell with his face still swollen.

"Two-fold," he said. "When Cash is informed that the weapons were hi-jacked by Taliban or insurgents—and not those Jaffri made the deal with—he'll be forced to look into other accommodations, or forced to return the money. Plus, we don't want him to know there's a rat. He'll suspect, but when questioned, his men will say they looked like Taliban. Gives us time."

"Still leaves the question of the drugs. Where's he taking delivery, and how's he planning to unload them?" Kyra inquired.

Taylor guided her back out into the hall, and they walked back the way they came. "Been to New York lately?"

Kyra glanced at him with raised eyebrows, curious.

"I have a stopover in London, but I'm scheduled to meet with Jaffri in New York next week. Why don't we ask him?"

"We?" she said.

Taylor gave her one of his winning smiles. "I'll be running the op; you'll merely be along as an observer." They arrived at the room where Tin and J.D. were veg'ing out on cots.

Taylor winked. "See you in New York."

Kyra gave Taylor a mock salute and walked through the door. "Give my regards to the boys at MI6."

CHAPTER 31

Karama, Dubai

Dressed in dark fatigues, LeClair stood on the rooftop with his eye behind a pair of night vision goggles, scoping out the area. The majority of residents worked early morning hours, so lights were out behind most curtains. He did one more sweep, stowed the goggles in his rucksack and tossed it over his shoulder then pulled a black balaclava down over his face so only his eyes and mouth were showing.

The building fifteen-stories tall, he secured a pair of rock-climbing ropes—one yellow, one blue—around a stone fixture that would hold his weight. After tying a double figure-8 Fisherman knot, he stepped into a harness and hooked the carabineer from the ropes, to the carabineer at his waist, and then walked backwards off the roof.

Planting his feet flat along the side of the building, he tightened the grip of his left-gloved hand on the yellow rope in front of him, and allowed the right-hand glove to loosen the blue allowing him to move. Then he rappelled down the side of the building, until he reached the top railing at the seventh floor.

He jumped down onto the balcony and landed softly on the concrete surface of the patio; the noise masked by the loud music coming from inside the

167

apartment. He quickly removed the carabineer, letting the ropes dangle along the side of the building. It was dark, so he knew nobody would see them, especially, since they wouldn't be looking for them.

He reached into the rucksack and retrieved the lock pick tool, and proceeded to slide the tool in between the frame and the sliding door, then twisted it counter-clockwise and lifted up until he heard the click.

He kept his eyes on the shadows moving around inside, as he reached for his Desert Eagle with a silencer. Then he slowly slid back the glass door, and stepped inside the room with the gun pointed.

The living room was clear, music played on the flat-screen TV on the wall. He moved down the hall, and glanced into the first door on the right. A woman was lying on the bed giggling with anticipation; her wrists tied to the bed posts, her eyes covered with a blindfold. LeClair shook his head. Hadley was at the opposite end of the room wearing a pair of red silk boxers, pouring two glasses of wine.

"Do you have a license for that alcohol?" LeClair mocked as he stepped into the room.

At the sight of the masked man with a gun, a guttural scream bellowed out of Hadley's throat. The noise caused Fuchs to burst through the door at the end of the hall.

LeClair turned the gun in his direction. A .50 caliber hollow point-tip round found its mark, right through the center of his forehead. Fuchs went down.

"Hadley?" the woman cried. "What's going on?"

Terrified, Hadley dropped the glasses. They shattered on the floor. He freaked, and backed up against the wall.

LeClair kept the gun on him, as he reached inside his rucksack and pulled out a blade. There was a gleam in his eyes at the sight of Hadley's horrified look as he sliced the knife through the ties that bound the woman to the bed. LeClair slipped the blindfold off her face, and gently wrapped the blanket around her, as he steered her toward the door.

Shaking in fear, but pissed off at the same time, she turned to Hadley and whined, "Last time there was a woman with a gun, and now there's a man in a mask? Why does this keep happening? What kind of man, are you?"

LeClair couldn't help himself, he chuckled. "My advice, find yourself a boyfriend who doesn't need to tie you up."

The woman screamed, suddenly seeing Fuch's dead body. She stared into LeClair's eyes.

"Go on," he told her, motioning for her to leave. She glanced toward Hadley once more; he looked like a terrified rabbit cornered in the room. She ran out of the bedroom, grabbed her handbag and clothes before she ran out the living room door.

LeClair then focused his eyes on Hadley.

Hadley shrank further into the corner, looking left and right for some kind of weapon. "Who are you? What do you want?"

LeClair motioned for Hadley to move over toward the silver attaché case. "Open it."

Hadley glanced toward the bedroom balcony window.

"Seven floors down. Odds aren't really in your favor," LeClair said, slightly amused. "You might make it, but you'll wind up with a few broken bones."

Realizing he had no choice, Hadley slowly moved toward the case, and opened it; the case still packed with hundred dollar bills.

"Take the money out, "LeClair ordered.

Hadley removed the money, and placed it down on the desk.

LeClair then reached his hand inside the case and removed the transmitter.

Hadley looked on, stunned. "How... I thought that was removed?"

LeClair motioned toward the money. "Never mind the transmitter. Put the money back in."

Hadley stacked the money back inside the case, fear riddled on his face.

"How much is there?" LeClair inquired.

Hadley hesitated. "Just shy of 250k."

LeClair closed the lid on the case. "You won't be needing it anymore." LeClair planted a bullet right between his eyes. Then he lifted the case and casually returned to the balcony, closing the sliding glass window behind him. He clipped the carabineer to the harness, stepped up onto the railing, and proceeded to rappel down to the ground.

He wasn't worried about the woman causing any trouble for him. In a conservative Arab country, she would need to explain why she was running around wrapped in a blanket with no clothes on underneath.

CHAPTER 32

Manhattan, New York
One week later

Kyra wore an off-the-shoulder red dress, with a simple pair of pearl earrings, a pair of tan sandals with a three-inch heel—putting her over six-feet-tall—and her hair loose down the middle of her back. She looked stunning sitting next to Taylor in a black Tuxedo, and a white, crisp shirt. Seated in the back seat of a black SUV with tinted windows, they traversed through the streets of Manhattan, headed toward the home of Tariq Jaffri.

ATU being a small unit with young agents, this was the first operation they took part in on American soil. Kyra only consented to tag along because Taylor informed her she would merely be observing.

Truthfully, she wanted to see Jaffri in person. She wanted to see what kind of man would live in the United States, be afforded the opportunity to acquire an education, financial prosperity and freedom, and yet, eagerly fund and provide weapons to the Taliban and insurgents with the whole intent to do harm to Americans.

She had trouble wrapping her head around that.

"So, who exactly, does this funder of terrorists think you are?"

Taylor turned to look at her, and smiled. It was a shame he had to use the ploy of an op to get her to go on a date with him. "Someone with a large shipping vessel, that if the deal is right, could help him transport his weapons and drugs anywhere in the world, and also has the connections to keep the Coast Guard and Customs off his back."

Kyra smiled, remembering their conversation back in his field office. "And, fearing another run in with insurgents or warlords stealing his weapons--?"

Taylor smiled back, and said, "The two-fold reason for keeping Jaffri's men alive."

"Does that shipping vessel have a name?"

Taylor glanced toward the Statue of Liberty. "Lady Liberty," he quipped.

Kyra's cellphone rang inside the small handbag she carried; she retrieved it and answered it. "Kyra Ray."

Tin was on the other end of the phone, talking a mile a minute, as usual. "Are you sitting down? Because if not, you should, because ... well, you're not going to believe this."

"Slow down, Tin."

Tin caught his breath, and started again. "Okay, J.D. and I were just coming back from dinner, so we decided to stop off at a sports bar and have a drink. Ya know, before hittin' the computer again. J.D. was heavy into the scenery. Lots of testosterone flowing in that boy, I tell you. I mean the guy has the girls throwing themselves at him, even though he still lives at home."

"Tin, focus," she said, getting confused trying to decipher what he was saying.

"Oh right, right. As I was saying, we were in the sports bar. Pretty cool place by the way. Anyway, I get a call from the home office, and they tell me to check the computer, so I did. And, well, your informant, Thomas Hadley... he was murdered."

"Murdered?" Kyra said, curious, but not really shocked by the news. You wind up dead when you play all sides. She glanced over at Taylor, who was busy checking his own messages. "Our asset, Thomas Hadley was murdered."

Before he could respond, she was back to speaking into the phone.

"Tin, do we know how?"

"He, and his bodyguard, both killed with a bullet to the forehead. Hadley was entertaining. The assassin allowed the girl to leave. Kyra, it could be the same guy that killed Agent Brady."

Kyra's knuckles clenched the phone. "What makes you say that?"

Tin said, ".50 caliber hollow point-tip round was retrieved from the bodies."

"That doesn't mean anything."

Tin interrupted her. "...and the second transmitter you placed in Hadley's case has been removed."

"Damn!" She said. She disconnected from the call. "I think Colton Cash Tate might be cleaning house."

***

LeClair sat aboard a Silverton Yacht that he rented and moored in the marina at the New York Harbor. He disliked hotels and preferred sleeping on boats where he could always hear who was coming.

In front of him, was the silver attaché case taken from Hadley. He removed the money then packed the bottom compartment with stacks of cheese loaded with C-4 plastiques, along with a timing device. He knew from his time in the boot camp training that explosives packed in cheese would be untraceable if they were to check him for wires or transmitters. Several packages of Opium were then stacked on top before he closed the lid.

CHAPTER 33

Manhattan, New York

When LeClair pulled the rented four-door Mercedes up to the front of Jaffri's brownstone, four armed guards surrounded the vehicle. They ordered him out, frisked him then demanded to see his identification. One checked his passport, while the others checked the vehicle for bombs.

They retrieved the attaché case from the passenger seat, waved a black wand over the case then quickly opened it, and looked inside.

They gave LeClair a smarmy smile at the sight of the Opium, closed the lid, then knowingly handed the case back to LeClair and cleared him to go inside.

LeClair walked up the steps to the brownstone as his eyes casually combed the street in a final security check. He stepped into the dark, wood floor lobby then was waved through by the man at the door after a nod from the guards outside.

In the hallway, he scanned the environment. Dark paneled walls with expensive Persian rugs, and antique chandeliers hung from the ceiling. A large living room was off to the right, but closed off by a set of French doors. A spiral staircase to his left, would take you to the second floor.

He heard men talking further down the hall then Jaffri, himself, exited a room on the left and walked towards him.

"You made it!" Jaffri said, wearing a phony smile as he extended a hand toward LeClair.

The two men shook hands, though it was a tense moment with both of them sizing each other up.

Jaffri's expression turned serious as he motioned down the hall. "Come, this way," he said.

LeClair followed him down the hall, entering a private office on the left with three other men. There, he scanned their faces, verifying that his targets were in the room.

The minute the office door closed behind him, Ahmed stood up from a chair by the window, and approached LeClair to frisk him.

LeClair gave Jaffri and Ahmed a smart-assed grin. "What, you don't trust your own guards outside?"

"Trust no one, you live longer," Jaffri said, with a smile. "Besides, a man in my position--"

LeClair glanced at both men in the room. He had no idea that Ahmed was an undercover MI6 agent, but believed him to be another funder of terrorists. In reality, he was just another target on Cash's hit list, a list that was going to pay enough money, so he could finally be free.

LeClair said, mockingly, "A man in your position should be more careful who he goes to bed with."

Jaffri shrugged. "And yet, here you are. You've brought something for me?"

LeClair set the attaché' case on top of the desk and opened it.

Jaffri picked up a package of the Opium then turned to his men. "Seems our friend Cash has come through for us."

He opened the bag, inspected the goods then placed it back in the case and shut the lid. "When will I take delivery of the rest?"

"Once security at the Harbor has been thoroughly vetted," LeClair said, authoritatively. "We wouldn't want you to lose the drugs, as you did the weapons."

Jaffri glowered at LeClair, and then his face cracked into a smile. "Ah yes, unfortunate setback, which I'm sure Cash will rectify."

"Yes, unfortunate," LeClair said, deadpan, knowing Cash would not be rectifying anything.

Jaffri placed the case down on the floor beside his desk with LeClair paying close attention, and then he looked to his men. "Now, we can continue with our plans. This will bring a fortune."

The men smiled, acknowledging their eagerness to begin.

Jaffri turned his attention back to LeClair. "Come, you must join us for dinner. We have some lovely guests here this evening that will be of great benefit to our future plans."

LeClair paused for a moment. He was not anticipating other guests, only the thugs involved with Jaffri. They were just collateral damage. Well, there was nothing he could do about it now, besides, if the new arrival was another player choosing to get involved with terrorists, LeClair wouldn't lose sleep over his demise.

"Another time perhaps; I have pressing business to attend to." He said eager to get out of there.

"Another time then," Jaffri said. "I expect word on the rest of my shipment as soon as possible."

LeClair gave him a curt nod. "As you wish."

Jaffri and the others escorted LeClair back into the lobby where they shook hands, and then LeClair left the building. Jaffri headed toward the dining room with his men following.

CHAPTER 34

Moments after LeClair and Jaffri disappeared into the private office, Kyra and Taylor arrived. After a thorough search by the guards out front, the door man escorted them into the dining area. Along the way, their eyes perused the brownstone, making sure they were aware of every escape route.

"Oops, forgot this," Taylor said, as he placed a hand on her arm motioning her to stop for a moment. He reached into his pocket, pulled out a gold wedding band, and discreetly handed it to her.

Kyra gave him a curious look.

"Can't have my darling wife be seen out in public without her wedding ring, now can I?"

"You told Jaffri I was your wife?"

Taylor leaned toward her and whispered into her ear. "Having you on my arm gives me the appearance of being trustworthy."

Kyra smirked. "Don't you mean makes you look good?"

"Ah c'mon, luv, you could do worse."

Kyra returned his grin. "But, I had hoped I could do better."

"Ouch!" Taylor said, playfully. "I get it, you're still sore I didn't tell you about my undercover with Jaffri."

"Being that we're allies," she said, as she discreetly slipped the ring on her finger. "Didn't know you were such a cheapskate, darling; make sure to add that to your dossier."

In a tongue-in-cheek kind of way, Taylor pinched her in the side, and continued with the banter. "Typical woman; they always turn bitchy once they get the ring."

Shaking her head, Kyra looped her hand through his arm and they filtered into the dining room. "Not true my handsome prince, I was bitchy long before you got down on one knee."

His head flew back in laughter, and then he got serious when Jaffri and company strode in through the door, and headed in their direction.

"Mr. Taylor," Jaffri said, extending a hand to Taylor, and noticing the bruises. "It's so good of you to join us this evening? What happened to your face?"

Taylor shrugged. "Blindsided during a rugby match."

Jaffri nodded, and then leered at Kyra. "And this must be your lovely wife. You didn't tell me she was so beautiful." Jaffri reached for Kyra's hand and kissed it.

"A lot of things he forgot to mention," Kyra whispered so only Taylor could hear.

While Jaffri continued to engage Kyra, Ahmed sent a private signal to Taylor, letting him know the Opium had arrived.

"He also forgot to mention that you were so charming," Kyra said, forcing a smile while his lips touched her skin.

Jaffri's eyes lit up, as he observed the two of them. "You two make a very handsome couple."

Taylor sported a smart-assed grin, as he turned to Kyra, and placed his arm around her and squeezed. "Wasn't I just telling you that earlier, luv?"

"Well, I'm not sure those were your exact words, darling," she said, sarcastically.

Jaffri said, "Come Taylor, meet my other associates." Jaffri guided them toward his other men.

As they walked, Kyra teasingly brushed up against Taylor. "You're enjoying this, aren't you?"

Taylor gave her a sarcastic smile. Jaffri quickly introduced Taylor to Ahmed and his other guards, and they began to chat.

Kyra excused herself for a moment, and ventured over to the buffet table for an appetizer, as well as get a feel for the room. Along the way, she kept a peripheral view on Jaffri. The man struck her as strange, living in a nice brownstone in Manhattan among various cultures. Reading his background, she knew he owned several convenient stores, started by money from the government, no doubt. Such hypocrisy, she thought to herself. When she returned to the group, the men were talking sports.

Jaffri said, "Seasons not going too good, so far; they're trailing their rivals, the Red Sox."

"Too bad about A-Rod leaving," Taylor said, trying to appear interested. "At least he could keep fans in the seats."

"Financially fruitful for the tabloids as well," Jaffri responded.

His men laughed and nodded in agreement, like puppets on a string, hanging on their bosses every word.

"I've never been a big fan of the Yankees, though," Jaffri admitted. "I prefer the Mets." He turned his attention to Kyra. "What about you, Mrs. Taylor? Are you a fan of baseball?"

"Not particularly," Kyra said, as she glanced at Taylor and grinned. "I prefer a game with a little more action and speed involved."

Jaffri smacked Taylor on the back, as if they were old chums. "That why she picked you, Taylor? You're an adrenaline junky, aren't you?"

Kyra pretended to snuggle up close to Taylor, as she whispered into his ear. "You do that quite well."

"Do what well?"

"Act chummy with a wannabe terrorist."

Taylor smiled, sardonically. "We do what we have to."

"If you gentlemen will excuse me, I need to freshen up," Kyra said. "Mr. Jaffri, could you please direct me?"

"Of course," he said. "You'll find a guest bathroom at the top of the stairs, and down to the right. That will give us men a moment to talk business. I'm sure you don't want us to bore you with such things."

Kyra nodded, and frowned as she walked away. Of course, they couldn't discuss business when she was around; she's a woman. She casually walked up the spiral stairs, pausing to admire the paintings of Pakistan on the wall.

At the top of the stairs, she turned to her right toward the restroom, but stopped in the doorway of a library with a set of French doors that opened to an outdoor terrace. Wanting to look at the view of the Manhattan skyline, she strolled outside.

She went to stand in the corner of the wrought-iron railing, mesmerized by the bright lights of New York City off in the distance. But as she looked around, her mind was instantly taken back to the events of September 11, 2001, staring at the new towers erected in place of the ones taken out by terrorists—like those that Tariq Jaffri associated himself with.

CHAPTER 35

A few blocks away, out of the eyesight of the guards, LeClair sat in his Mercedes, keeping his eye on his watch. The second hand moved; almost time. A knowing smile crossed his face, realizing he would have enough money to buy himself an island somewhere and break away.

He glanced back at Jaffri's brownstone and noticed a woman standing on the balcony, staring out at the view. He would know her anywhere, an exquisite vision with her dark hair flowing in the breeze, and the woman whose blue eyes kept invading his dreams. Her presence shocked him to the core as the realization dawned on him. She was not supposed to be there.

"No!" LeClair uttered.

He bolted out of the car and ran toward the building, waving his hands in the air and screaming at the top of his lungs, trying to get her attention, and not caring that it would alert the guards.

Before he could reach her, the building erupted in multiple explosions, throwing LeClair to the ground.

Glass shattered.

Debris, concrete and metal flew in every direction.

The guards pummeled to the ground.

The blast knocked Kyra off the balcony. She flew through the air, and landed on top of an SUV.

When the rumbling finally subsided, there was a massive hole in the middle of the building, impossible for many to survive.

Glass, debris and rubble covered the street. LeClair slowly pulled himself up out of the clutter, suffering from minor scratches, he ran in Kyra's direction.

From his vantage point, she lay motionless, covered with cuts and abrasions, and a big gash across her leg.

Reaching her, he checked her vitals then carefully lifted her off the SUV, and gently placed her down on the ground.

Hearing the sirens wailing in the distance, he tilted her head back, pinched her nose and began to breathe air into her lungs. He pressed his hand down on her chest, and pumped.

"C'mon, c'mon," He pleaded, his voice frantic.

He pinched her nose again and pumped air until she started to cough.

With the sirens closing in, LeClair leaned her up against the SUV. He traced his fingers across her face then kissed her forehead.

"Please forgive me," he said, in a voice riddled with emotion. He had no idea why this woman touched his soul. Knowing help was on the way, he raced back toward the Mercedes, jumped in and burned rubber down the street.

Simultaneously, patrol cars and fire engines barreled onto the chaotic scene.

***

In the pre-dawn hours, first responders and law enforcement personnel sifted through the rubble, collecting evidence, while paramedics transported the injured victims to the hospital. Those that were deceased were lying on the ground with white sheets draped over their lifeless bodies.

Barry West and a diplomat from the British Embassy in New York stood over two bodies. The Medical Examiner pulled back the white sheet to show their faces: the remains of Logan Taylor and the man they knew as Ahmed.

"Are these two yours?" West said in a monotone voice.

The Diplomat nodded with a solemn expression.

West mused on the fact that it was never easy, being the person delivering the news of a death. He took this hit just as personal as he did the loss of Mike Brady. MI6 was an ally in the war on terror. He didn't know Ahmed, but Logan Taylor was a friend; a good agent. They attended some of the same training sessions. He raked a hand through his hair, trying to make sense of this latest hit. How did Kyra keep surviving?

Several hours later, Kyra was lying in a bed at Mount Sinai Hospital with an IV protruding from her arm. She had a bandage wrapped around her head from the fall. She was battered and bruised, but she was alive, miraculously. She suffered a concussion, and was in and out of consciousness throughout the night, but the worst was over, according to the doctor. The last thing she remembered was walking out onto the terrace.

"How did it happen," Kyra mumbled, barely able to find her voice and going through a ton of emotions.

Barry West sat in a chair next to her bed with a look of concern on his face. "Investigation is ongoing, but they believe explosives were placed in the bottom of an attaché case that was used to deliver the Opium. They discovered it in Jaffri's private office on the first floor, where the impact centered. Expecting delivery of the opium, I'm guessing that Jaffri's guards didn't do their due diligence."

Kyra's face was a mask of confusion, shock and anger. "And it blew, just as I happened to be outside?"

"Since we don't know, yet, who carried in the explosives, we don't know the target. Then again, it could be just a coincidence that you were outside."

"But we know agents keep dying, yet I keep surviving!"

CHAPTER 36

Operations Center, ATU
Two Days Later

"I was able to retrieve this from one of the surveillance video-cameras in the area," J.D. said to West. "They're hidden all over New York City."

"You've already seen the footage?" West asked J.D.

"Both of us have."

Tin slipped a flash drive into the computer, while West and J.D. stood behind him with their eyes on the monitor. Tin typed a few keys into the keyboard then video images appeared on the screen.

"Shows the surrounding area around Jaffri's brownstone at the appointed times" Tin added.

On the screen, a dark Mercedes pulled up to the building, immediately surrounded by the guards. LeClair stepped out.

"This guy shows up minutes before Kyra and Taylor's arrival to the Brownstone."

Pointing toward something on the screen, J.D. said, "Now look, the guards remove an attaché case from his car, check it and hand it to him."

On the screen, they watched LeClair enter the brownstone. Tin fast-forwarded the footage to where Kyra appeared on the second-floor terrace. "Here's our girl."

"Pause it right there," J.D. said.

Once Tin had the video paused, J.D. pointed toward the corner of the screen. "The Mercedes is parked right there. A little over two blocks away. Go ahead, Tin."

Tin pushed play. "The mystery guy gets out of the Mercedes..."

They watched the mystery man race toward the building. They heard the explosion on the video before they saw it, but they see Kyra fly off the terrace.

"Look what he does after," Tin said, shaking his head in confusion.

They watched as LeClair picked himself up out of the debris and rubble, make his way over to Kyra, and then immediately check her vitals. He lifted her off the SUV, placed her down on the ground and proceeded to breathe life back into her.

J.D. said, "When he was sure she was alive, he leaned her up against the SUV for the rescue workers to find her then jumped back into his Mercedes, and sped away from the scene."

Tin said, "He saved her life."

The three of them looked at each other, totally stunned by what they saw.

West frowned. "Do we know who this guy is?"

Tin shook his head. "No, trying to I.D. him now."

"Our assumption is he's the elusive assassin," J.D. said. "Up until now, all we had to track him was the bank account in Zurich."

Tin added, "Now, we have a face. Where do you think he got that scar?"

J.D. shrugged. "Maybe one of his victims fought back, before he snuffed the life out of them."

"Keep at it," West ordered. "I want you working non-stop until we know what connection this man has to our girl, and I want it yesterday."

Tin's fingers were already busy at the task, working his magic. "I'm going to need some more espresso."

West ran his fingers through his hair, a myriad of thoughts going through his head. "How's she doing today, have you talked to her?"

J.D. said, "Surprisingly well. Miraculous she didn't have any broken bones. The Doc gave her the all clear; so I'll be driving to New York to bring her home. She didn't want to fly."

Tin said, "Only seen that happen one other time. Well, I didn't actually see it, but heard about it. Guy jumped out of a high-rise, fell fifteen stories down, and walked away from it. They said it was because he was drunk and his body was relaxed, but how could that be? I mean, does that mean our girl's body was relaxed at the time she flew off the terrace?"

Tin looked around, only to realize the room had emptied out while he was babbling. He shrugged, switched his baseball cap around and turned back to the computer. His eyes focused on the screen as a number of images scanned on the right, hoping to locate a match to the image of the mystery man on the left.

Back at the Mount Sinai Hospital, Kyra slept while LeClair stood in the shadows of the hospital room, watching her, making sure she was alive.

CHAPTER 37

Two days later, Tin jerked to attention when the computer flashed an image that matched the face of LeClair from the explosion at the embassy. He and J.D. had been working around the clock scanning thousands of images, while he and J.D. took turns dozing off at a desk nearby.

Tin slapped the bottom of J.D.'s boot to get his attention. "Think I've got him!" Tin shouted.

J.D. slowly stirred awake and looked at the images on the screen; the recent image on the left with the scar, and a passport photo before the scar.

"Think we've got us a winner."

Tin pressed a button and almost instantly, a dossier for Dalton LeClair appeared on the screen. He breezed through it. "There's nothing here. All this says is that he was born in Canada, wound up in Florida with a set of foster parents who were killed when he was nineteen."

"This is helpful," J.D. said, motioning toward a section on the dossier. "Says he attended a boot camp with former Delta Force members were the instructors."

Tin stared at him. "How is that helpful?"

J.D. shrugged. "Only a couple boot camps like that around. Delta Force doesn't advertise their expertise, and they aren't cheap. You have to know people to get an invite. Let me make a few calls." He disappeared over to his desk.

Tin took the time to wander out into the hall to the vending machine. He needed some caffeine. Looking through the options, he settled on an Iced Tea, and bought a couple of *Hershey's* dark-chocolate bars. He finished one of the bars, and then returned to his desk.

When J.D. rejoined him about a half-hour later, he was wearing a frown. "Talked to a guy down in Florida; he was the original owner of a boot camp down there. Anyway, I told him what I was looking for. At first, he clammed up, until I told him about the dead agents. Story he told me paints a different picture of Dalton LeClair.

"Said Colton Cash Tate paid a hefty fee so LeClair could attend the boot camp when he was around drinking age, so he must have been twenty-one or so. Delta guys said he excelled at training; would have fit right in on any team. Only problem was, LeClair thought he was being trained and hired as a personal bodyguard."

"Well, it's not like an assassin goes around announcing what he does," Tin said.

"That's true," J.D. continued. "But these Delta guys said it didn't go down like that. Said LeClair disappeared right after he finished the camp, even though they became friendly and made plans to get a few beers.

"Deltas didn't think much of it; then they heard a rumor in a mercenary forum that The Chechen was bragging about leaving a scar on a young kid getting brainwashed to work for his boss. They don't use names in the forums, but everybody knows who is who. Delta guy said he did a little digging and sure enough, he heard about the hit man with a scar on Cash's personal payroll."

Tin looked confused. "Okay, so Cash paid for his training?"

J.D. nodded. "I think what the Deltas were trying to tell me was that LeClair was an unwitting assassin. The way I read it; Cash and The Chechen beat him into submission."

Tin shook his head. "Well, if he's an assassin, why not just kill Cash and The Chechen?"

J.D. shrugged. "That's what I can't figure. Who knows what Cash has on him now? It's like *Jason Bourne*, you get brainwashed in a way."

Tin thought about it. "Maybe, but I doubt Kyra will care about the why, only that he killed her fellow agents."

CHAPTER 38

Ops Center, ATU

West sat at the head of the conference table observing Kyra's reaction while Tin replayed the video images of the explosion. The minute LeClair's image showed on the monitor, Kyra moved in for a closer look; her face riddled with confusion. She watched as he lifted her off the SUV and proceeded to give her CPR.

"I've seen him before," Kyra said.

West raised his eyebrows at her. "Where?"

Her head still fuzzy, she paused to think about the last two weeks' events, and then her eyes lit up at the realization. "I couldn't swear to it; I thought I caught a glimpse of him on Cash's yacht. But I know with a hundred percent certainty that he was in Afghanistan; I saw those eyes when he held a gun to my head, and chose not to shoot."

West, Tin and J.D. glanced at each other with stunned expressions on their faces.

"He had you in his crosshairs, but chose not to shoot?" West said, stunned. "And why in the hell is this the first time I'm hearing about that?"

Kyra averted her eyes and shook her head, reeling from the confusion. "I don't know. At the time, I couldn't understand it; why he let me live. Then, I was afraid. You heard Thompson and Sanger; they thought I was in collusion."

"Those piss-ants don't concern me, Kyra, this group in here, we are a team." He let out a heavy sigh. "Never mind, we'll deal with that later. You saw him in the UAE?"

She nodded. "I noticed him on the yacht, staring at me when I was approached by a man in Armani who asked me to dance. I declined, of course."

"Of course," Tin said, joking.

Kyra shot a glance his way.

West said, "Well ... it appears our assassin has taken an interest in you."

Kyra's brows furrow. "That's ridiculous. We've never even had a conversation."

Tin smiled. "Maybe it was a fleeting glance."

J.D. added, "Sparks, a chemical reaction."

"Who needs words when you have a powerful physical attraction?" Tin threw in for good measure.

Tin and J.D. knowingly nodded as if it made perfect sense, while Kyra looked at them as if they were crazy.

Kyra said, "Our encounters, if you could call them that, were brief, almost non-existent."

"It's seduction of the purest kind," Tin offered. "The adrenaline surges, sending a rush of serotonin to the brain, and then mixing in the pheromones of a beautiful woman."

Kyra shook her head at him, and then looked around at all three of the men in the room who were staring at her. "Are you telling me this assassin became infatuated with me to the point he killed other agents, but felt compelled to save me because of self-indulgent lust from afar?"

"Pure unadulterated sexual magnetism," J.D. said, smiling as if he understood it all too well.

West's reaction turned serious. "Look Kyra, there may be more to it than that, or maybe that's exactly what it is. It is not farfetched for a man to have an instant chemical reaction to a woman. Either way, there is a reason this man keeps saving your life, which tells me you may be able to use that knowledge to your advantage."

Kyra was taken aback. "How ... wait, you're not suggesting..."

Tin and J.D. looked at each other, and smiled.

J.D. said, "Honeypot; using her sexual wares."

Kyra's facial expression went from a look of uncertainty to one tinged with anger at the realization of what they were suggesting she do.

"On the man that killed three agents? Please tell me you're just hypothesizing here."

"On the contrary," West said, deadpan. "I'm dead serious."

She narrowed her eyes and glared at West. "Weren't you the one that said--"

Tin and J.D. interrupted her, speaking in unison. "If a man can rely on a woman more for her qualities of companionship, than those of physical satisfaction..."

West threw his hand in the air, advising them to stop. "Enough! I know what I said."

Kyra stared at the images of LeClair on the computer screen; the passport photo of him before the scar, and the current image of him saving her life. Even with the scar, she had to admit he was devastatingly handsome with his dark hair, almost black, the muscled physique, and the tanned skin from obviously living most of his life outdoors. But even without the knowledge that he was an assassin, he had the look of someone who was dangerous. It was his eyes. There was an intensity to them; eyes that could see through to her soul. She remembered them all too well when he held a gun to her head, and the heat penetrated through her. He was the type of man she would steer clear of if she were living a normal life, and out there in the dating world—a life she gave up due to memories of her past and choosing the life of an operative. That kind of life was not in the cards for Kyra. She finally let out a heavy sigh. "What's the bottom line here?"

West stared at her with an intensity she has never seen before. "You are to use whatever means necessary to get close to the targets then take them down."

There was an audible gasp in the room from Tin and J.D.

"So, you want me to take them out. You're giving me a sanction to kill?"

West cocked his head to the side, giving her the affirmative, without actually saying it.

CHAPTER 39

Kyra peered out the window of a private Cessna airplane. The bandages were now gone, but some of the bruises remained, though fading. Through the thick clouds, she got a glimpse of the private airstrip just over the Blue Ridge Mountains. Her body jolted as the wheels touched down and the plane taxied over to a waiting SUV.

She stepped off the plane carrying her duffel bag and took a brief moment to breathe in the fresh air, and enjoy the scenery.

Sergeant Mark McBride, a no-nonsense, ex-military man stepped out of the SUV to greet her. He offered his hand in a firm handshake, then grabbed up her bag. "Welcome to my palace," he said. "Names Mark, but folks here call me Sarge."

Kyra returned the shake. "Thanks, Kyra."

Sarge guided her toward the vehicle. "Enjoy the ride over?"

"It was a little rocky," Kyra said.

"Probably turbulence over the mountains," he said. "The air is thicker up here." At the SUV, Sarge politely opened the front passenger door for her. He placed her bag in the back, then returned to the driver's side and hopped in.

Within a few minutes they were driving up a bumpy gravel road, further into the hills. Kyra was overwhelmed by the mountains in the distance. "Scenery's beautiful up here. You must really enjoy it?"

Sarge took a moment to look around at the view. "Don't get much time to enjoy, but do when we can."

"So, do you know why Barry West and my Uncle Ray conspired to send me here?" Kyra inquired.

Sarge gave her a side-ways glance, surprised she would even ask. "They sent you here, because agents are dead. You suffered some injuries, but you've still got a job to do. We don't mess around when it comes to prepping our people for the job at hand. Got a lot to do, and little time to do it."

Kyra glanced in the side-view mirror and watched the private plane as it got further and further away. "Guess I better get myself into game mode then."

"Or wind up like the others," Sarge said, speaking frankly.

"Dead!" Kyra said in a grave voice.

He pulled up to a row of cabins, stopped the SUV and hopped out. Grabbed her duffel bag from the back seat then opened the door to number two, and set the duffel on the floor inside.

"Should have what you need," he said. "Anything else; I'll be at the house down yonder." He pointed to a two-story log home several hundred feet down the hill. Take the rest of the day to get acclimated, chows on at

201

0800 in the a.m. then we'll hit the ground running. He disappeared down the road.

She walked into the cabin, noticing the musty smell. First thing she did was open the windows to let in the air. Then she took her clothes out of the duffel—mostly workout gear—and placed them in the drawers of a small bureau. She opened a small refrigerator to find cases of water, Gatorade, and protein bars inside.

Feeling antsy, she put on a pair of sweats and a tank top then slipped into her running shoes. After putting her hair into a ponytail, she opened the door, and started slowly jogging down the hill.

A couple hours later, she was trying to make it back up the dirt hill; sweating profusely and determined to get to the top, but struggling in a way she never had.

"C'mon," Sarge ordered, following her up in the rear and not even breaking a sweat. "Pick up your feet."

Kyra gave it everything she could, but her feet were laden with lead.

"Move your ass!" Sarge shouted at her.

"Jesus, I just got here, can't you ease up a bit," she whined back at him. "I didn't ask you to tag along."

"Oh, stop your whining; we don't have time for babies here on my land."

Kyra gritted her teeth and pushed herself to continue, if for no other reason than to get away from her new drill sergeant.

At 0800 the following morning, they sat down to a plate of scrambled eggs with spinach, sliced tomatoes, two English muffins, and a glass of fresh-squeezed juice. They ate in silence.

When they finished, a housekeeper cleared the table and did the dishes, while he sat her down on the Farmer's Porch and told her what was going to happen over the next few days. Got a job to do, and little time to do it, he repeated.

After enough time passed for the food to digest, they went to the barn where he gave her a pair of boxing gloves and ordered her into the ring. He gave her a few minutes to warm up and get into the groove, but then he climbed into the ring with her, and clocked her within a few minutes.

They did that song and dance for a couple hours.

With her ego officially bruised, he continued to pile on her in drill instructor mode, ordering her to do two hundred sit-ups, pulls-ups, and push-ups.

"Each?" she said, glaring at him.

"This ain't cheerleading camp, lady," he spat out at her, disappointed in the lack of gung ho attitude.

Military boot camp and operative training was a long time ago, and even though she exercised daily, she wasn't sure she could do it. She surprised herself and pushed through it, but it took a while and she whined along the way—a major, no, no—which got her another fifty.

For three days, they exercised, sparred, jogged, and then exercised again. They did a couple hours of martial arts in the afternoons, and then an hour with the KA-

Bar. She got a little cocky then, she was always lucky with the blades.

He brought her back down to earth rather quickly, when it was time to run again. For the girl who used to be able to run for miles, she was struggling to get up the hills, and he was always right there to point it out. It occurred to her that the explosion made her a little congested, so she started a little breathing meditation to bring in some oxygen.

At 2000 hours on the fourth day, they stopped for some chow then he sent her up to her cabin, and told her to get some shuteye, and report at 0400 hours in the morning. When she groaned, he gave her a lazy smile, and said, "Got lots to do and little time to do it."

Kyra returned to the room, grabbed a bottle of water from the refrigerator, and went to sit on the cot. A stack of photographs was lying on top. Rifling through the first few, her body tensed up: the dead body of Mike Brady, the burned out remnants of the Tariq Jaffri's building, and the dead bodies of Logan Taylor and Ahmed, and then finally, the images of Colton Cash Tate and Dalton LeClair.

It occurred to her that her Uncle Ray put the photographs in the hands of the Sarge, so they could play a little mind game. Instead of getting irritated, she sat down on the cot and stared at the photos until the images burned into her soul.

CHAPTER 40

The following morning, it was like something, or somebody, possessed her. She hurried through the morning chow, helped the housekeeper clean up, and pushed Sarge to get moving, and not the other way around. Breathing a little more oxygen helped.

Consumed with anger and determination, she breezed through a military-style obstacle course. She jumped up to a bar to do pull-ups, waded through a foot of mud, crawled under a chain of wire, hurdled through rings of tires, feet-first on top of a six-foot wall, climbed over and jumped to the bottom, and then continued running up the dirt road. Even Sarge admitted it was impossible to get in her way. "Finally, a compliment," she teased.

"I'm not in the compliment business," Sarge said, shaking head with disappointment. "Now, because you're starting to get cocky, do it again."

Throwing her hands up in defeat, she forced her body through another obstacle course, but this time when she reached the finish, she kept her big mouth shut. She could have sworn she caught the glimpse of a smile on the ole' Sarge's face.

Later on, Kyra stood in a cubicle at the firing range checking over her Sig Sauer P226 and 9mm ammo. She donned a pair of goggles and put in ear guards, planted her feet then aimed toward the target fifty feet away. She fired one, then another, both of them a little off. She took in a breath and then fired another, better, so she started firing one after the other until she was out of ammo. Reloaded the weapon and went at it again, trying to relieve the pent up tension from the last few weeks. She went at it for hours, and then again the next few days, until Sarge was sure she didn't lose her touch and wasn't afraid to pull the trigger when it was time.

After lunch during her second week there, the two of them headed to the barn, but this time Sarge led her into a back room with wall-to-wall shelves of surveillance, electronics and high-tech spy equipment.

He sat her down at a desk and went over a few of the items. Recorders, radios, compacts used for surveillance, lipstick bombs, pen explosives, and various others. They talked weapons, the different types of grenades—flash bang and stun.

While he had her talking, he asked her about her time as a prisoner. Did they keep her with the men? How bad was the torture? What got her through it? When he asked her about being raped, she didn't deny it, but he didn't call too much attention to it either, which made it easier for her to open up. A bond formed between instructor and student. But what she also realized was that him getting her to talk about her past, the rape and torture, was all part of the plan. By opening the flood gates of her emotions, in a nonthreatening way, he was making it easier for her to move past it, and accept what she ultimately had to do.

To add a little levity after the sombre conversation, Sarge grabbed a tech device off of the desk, and showed it to her.

Kyra took the device in her hand then laughed. "Is this a tampon?"

Sarge grinned. "Looks like it, don't it?"

She examined it, while Sarge quietly observed.

"It's a transmitter," he finally said, when she still looked stumped.

Then surprise crossed her face. "A transmitter? People wear these?"

Sarge dismissed her shock with a wave of the hand. "Kyra, female spies have been around for centuries; if the situation called for it, women donned transmitters in places men wouldn't think to check."

Intrigued, Kyra analyzed the contraption, tried to take it apart to see how it worked.

"Pull string's the antennae," Sarge pointed out.

Kyra gave him a look, with a snide smile. "If I was wearing that thing and I happen to be on the rag, wouldn't that short it out?"

The rough and tough Sarge didn't even blush at her bold statement. "Won't affect it, wise guy."

Kyra thought about the next phase of her mission, and quickly analyzed how the equipment Sarge was showing her might be useful. Then her lips curved into a smile when another thought occurred to her. "What's the possibility of arming this with explosives?"

The old cantankerous Sarge couldn't help himself, he laughed. "Shit girl, don't make me piss my pants."

CHAPTER 41

Seated behind the wheel of a Rubicon Jeep, Kyra raced like a demon up a windy, dirt road. Sarge locked himself behind the seatbelt and held on, as he jostled about in the passenger seat. It was supposed to be a defensive driving course, but Kyra already took that class in her operative training, so she was bored.

She happened upon a sharp turn, and didn't bother to slow down, taking the turn at full speed.

"Okay, hotshot," Sarge said. "I get it. You take after the General; just so happens he had a need for speed, too."

"You two served together?" Kyra asked, mildly surprised. From the time she was a young girl, he was her Uncle Ray, but to everyone else he was always the General.

"You could say that," Sarge said, not elaborating, and leaving her to wonder in what capacity.

She glanced over at him and smiled, ready to fire off a round of questions, before she heard the ring of her cell phone. Knowing it was probably ATU she slowed down and picked up the phone. "Kyra Ray," she shouted when answering.

"You're not going to believe what I'm looking at," Tin said on the other end.

"Tell me."

While Kyra was in the mountains being reacquainted with her skills as well as learning a few new ones, Tin and J.D. were trying to locate the whereabouts of Colton Cash Tate and Dalton LeClair. Through his sources at the air base in the UAE, J.D. learned that The Sahara left the marina at Yas Island two days after they rescued Taylor.

"I've got our mystery boy on camera," Tin continued. "He just checked in on an International Air flight at Los Angeles International Airport."

Kyra whipped the jeep over to the side of the road. "LAX? You sure it's him, Tin?" He risked his own freedom saving her life in New York by exposing himself to the security cameras along the streets; why would a trained assassin jeopardize himself, again?

"He's taking measures to avoid the camera," Tin continued, "but it's him. Hang on, and I'll give you the name he's using and his itinerary."

Even using an alias and hiding his face, he knows the danger. Does he want us to find him?

Kyra's mind raced as she tried to digest the new information and how she was going to use it to implement a plan of attack.

Tin came back on the line. "He's using the alias, Anthony Burgess. He went by motor boat from New York to Los Angeles then booked himself on a flight leaving for London. From there, he connects to a flight heading to Zurich."

Kyra frowned. "Zurich?" Then she remembered Tin telling her early on that Cash had a hideaway Chateau in Zurich. That was probably where he escaped to when he was feeling a little heat.

"What are the odds he's going for a meet and greet with Cash?" Tin suggested.

"Maybe to collect his final payoff," Kyra responded through clenched teeth.

Without alerting Sarge, Kyra did a quick U-turn, spinning the tires and kicking up a cloud of dust. Caught off guard, he grabbed a hold of the door handle.

"Tin, keep your eye on him. Make sure he gets on that flight. If there's any change, let me know, immediately. Oh, and Tin... clear it with West, but have J.D. put together a surveillance team to meet that plane. I need eyes on him 24/7."

She clicked off the phone, and the look of determination returned.

"Sorry Sarge, my time with you has come to an end."

CHAPTER 42

Zurich, Switzerland

A few years ago, Kyra took a vacation that had her driving all the way from Southern California, stopping long enough to enjoy a day at the gorgeous beaches, and then continuing on up into the mountains. There was only one road to get there, Pacific Coast Highway, and it was miles and miles of winding, coastal road, similar to the one Kyra was driving on now, taking her up into the mountains of Zurich.

She had been driving the rented Mini-Cooper for several miles; the ten-inch wheels expertly taking the curves. Her mind was on business, but she couldn't help but admire the view, just like her trip through California.

There was no traffic on the road, and only one destination at the end: a contemporary chateau, which sat alone at the top of the mountain, surround by water on all sides, but one, and was owned by none other than illegal arms dealer, Colton Cash Tate.

The private Chateau was originally one of many homes owned by a legendary rock musician who finally settled down and married when he turned sixty, and then sold off his vacation spots to purchase a sprawling estate in Paris, France. When Cash got his hands on the property, he had his architects tear down the original structure and rebuild to his new specifications.

"Guys, I'm getting bored," Kyra said into the hidden mic when she looked at the road ahead and realized there were still several more miles to go. "Can't you at least talk about something, or turn on some tunes?"

"What are we, your free entertainment?" J.D. joked.

"Yeah, tell me about your latest hook up," she said. "That usually sparks some interesting stories."

Tin laughed. "Yes J.D., do tell her about your latest tryst when mommy and daddy walked in on you."

"Shut up, Tin," J.D. said.

"Your parents walked in on you having sex?"

"We weren't having sex, exactly."

"Oh, do tell," she said, eager to hear the humorous details. At that same moment, she spotted a pair of headlights in her rear-view mirror. "Hold that thought guys I've got a dark-colored Mercedes coming up behind me."

"Dude, you really do need to get your own place," Tin said, keeping the conversation going.

"Yeah, yeah," J.D. responded.

The Mercedes was gaining speed and starting to get close.

"Guys, I know I said I wanted entertainment, but right now I really need to focus."

Then a second pair of headlights, belonging to a Citroen C-4, sped up and passed the Mercedes on the opposite side of the road, and continued toward her.

"Got me a double whammy here guys," she said, as she mentally prepared herself. "I think they're hostiles, and they're coming on strong."

Keeping her eyes on the road ahead, she noticed only one occupant in the Citroen C-4 through her peripheral view.

The Citroen continued until it was almost directly opposite the Mini, then at the same time, the Mercedes rammed into the rear bumper of the Mini.

"Definitely hostiles," she said, as her heart rate accelerated.

She glanced in the rear-view mirror saw two men in the front seat of the Mercedes, possibly more in the back, and the front-seat passenger held the barrel of a sub-machine gun in front of him.

"I've got a Citroen C-4 boxing me in on my left, the Mercedes ramming my bumper, and the front passenger armed with a submachine gun."

"Oh shit," Tin said.

"No kidding," Kyra responded.

The Mercedes bumped the rear of the mini, again. Then suddenly, a squeeze move from the Citroen, causing the metal to grind and sparks to fly.

Tires on the mini squealed, as Kyra downshifted and held her own. She quickly sized up her surroundings.

If she swerved to the right, she would drop seventy feet off the mountain and into the water. Attempting to go left meant a drive up a steep embankment; that is if she could get around the Citroen. The Mini did have speed and maneuverability on its side.

At the next tap from the Mercedes, Kyra accelerated and turned the wheel to the left, forcing the mini into the Citroen – which barely made a dent.

The driver of the Citroen punched the gas, pulling directly in front of the mini, blocking her in between both vehicles. The crunch of metal drowned out the squeal of the tires.

The driver of the Citroen slammed on the brakes, and lurched to a sideways skid, just as the Mercedes slowed.

With that, Kyra made her move. She downshifted as she hit the brake then cranked the wheel to the left. As the nose of the mini broke free, Kyra hit the gas and tore up the embankment.

CHAPTER 43

Through the rear view mirror Kyra watched both cars come to a sudden halt. The two men seated in the front seat of the Mercedes, jumped out. At the same time, the driver of the Citroen did the same.

Simultaneously, all three men planted their feet in the pavement, and aimed their weapons toward the mini.

Kyra ducked, as bullets ripped through the back window and shattered the glass.

The sub-machine gun riddled holes into the fiberglass body, shattering the brake lights and piercing through the bumper.

Just when she made it halfway up the embankment, the rear wheels of the mini lost their traction. The tires started to skid backwards and the mini started to move back down the hill.

Knowing she would be mincemeat if she faced the men and their weapons, Kyra dove out of the car and grabbed hold of the bushes and rocks. While she hung on with all her might, the mini rolled back down the embankment.

Thinking she was still in the car, the three shooters peppered the mini with rounds of bullets, as it rolled towards them. Then it came to a dead stop once it was back on the road.

Shooter number #1 took a quick look inside the mini and noticed it was empty. He flashed his Maglite up the embankment.

"She got out," he yelled to the others. "Up there, on the hill."

The others immediately turned their weapons in her direction. A barrage of bullets whipped past her head.

She flattened out on her belly behind a boulder, whipped out her gun and fired two shots in the direction of the Citroen, hoping to hit the driver. He immediately rolled out of the way.

The sub-machine gun chattered to life as the passenger from the Mercedes unloaded it up in Kyra's direction, sending rock chips and dirt flying down on her shoulders.

"Fuck!" She muttered to herself. She made a quick beeline toward another set of rocks, and ducked low behind them, keeping herself hidden in the dark of night.

When the chattering stopped, she heard the sound of a boot crunch against the scrub, as the driver of the Mercedes attempted to climb up the embankment.

Kyra put her sights on the driver of the Citroen; pre-occupied reloading his weapon. She aimed, took the shot and watched him go down.

The chatter of the sub-machine gun started up again. Bullets shattered the earth all around the rocks where she was hiding. She curled up into a fetal position to keep from being hit, and then fired back, making the Mercedes passenger stop firing and take immediate cover.

She laid down on her back and kept her gun pointed forward, listening for the driver of the Mercedes. She froze when she heard footsteps directly above the rocks where she was hiding, but was grateful that he couldn't see her.

The passenger from the Mercedes yelled up to the driver, "Now! She's right below you!"

The driver started to fire several rounds near the rocks where she was hiding, but she rolled away from the line of fire.

Then luck was on her side, for a brief second his body silhouetted in the moonlit sky: Kyra pumped two slugs dead center to his chest. There was a gargled scream as his body sailed down the embankment.

Not knowing who it was, the passenger of the Mercedes fired the sub-machine gun at the tumbling body.

Kyra took advantage of the situation. She aimed her weapon toward the orange flame of the sub-machine gun, and fired several rounds. The passenger spun around then dropped face down onto the hood of the Mercedes. His last screams echoed in the night.

CHAPTER 44

Filled with a new-founded burst of adrenaline, Kyra quickly made her way back down the embankment to the mini. Surprisingly, it was still running. She jumped in and continued her course toward the chateau.

"Well, that was fun," she said, sarcastically, thankful to be alive.

Her moment of thanks was fleeting when she felt the cold steel of a Beretta 92SB aimed at her temple.

"Does this mean the ride's over?" Kyra mused, feeling like she just completed one hell-of-a roller coaster ride only to be tossed out at the end.

Then her body trembled with fear when The Chechen rose up out of the back seat.

"Drive!" He said, as his predatory eyes stared back at her through the rear-view mirror.

"You're not still mad at me, are you?" She said, trying to keep a little levity in her voice, and at the same time, alert Tin and J.D. to the situation.

The Chechen responded by pulling the earpiece out of her ear then leaned over and yanked the transmitter.

"Ouch! I guess you are."

He rolled the window down, and dropped them outside.

"You know that blade in your chest was nothing personal."

"Stop Talking!"

"Not the talkative kind, huh?"

"I said drive," he ordered, pushing the Beretta harder against her temple.

"Okay, okay, so you don't like chatter. I get it. Sorry, I tend to talk when I get nervous." Now I know how Tin feels, she thought to herself. She stepped on the gas, and kept him in her sights through the rear-view mirror.

When the Mini reached the top of the mountain, The Chechen ordered her to turn right onto a decorative paved road that curved around in a winding spiral for about a mile. The road came to a stop at a gate that parted upon their arrival, and opened to a circular driveway with a helipad in the center.

"Drive," The Chechen ordered.

Kyra continued through the gate, pulling the Mini around to the front of the house.

"Out," he said. He kept the gun aimed at her with one hand, and reached up to the passenger seat and grabbed her duffel bag.

She slowly stepped out of the car, and moved forward with the motion of the gun. He ushered her to a side door entrance, and pushed her through the door.

***

On the side of the mountain, directly underneath the chateau, two lights flicked on and then off.

CHAPTER 45

Piloting a Robinson R22 Beta Helicopter, LeClair circled over the area surrounding the chateau—the whump – whump - whump sound of the rotor blade slicing through the air putting the guards watching the perimeter immediately on alert. Maneuvering the chopper to the northern side, he hovered a good hundred feet above the mountain, counting down the seconds, then two lights suddenly flicked on and off. Satisfied, he set the chopper down on the helipad; the landing kicking up a cloud of dust, and pissing off the guards. After shutting down the engine, he stepped outside and smiled at the first guard who thrust a weapon to his chest.

"Easy there," he said, with a calm demeanor. "I believe your boss is expecting me."

The guard stepped forward and proceeded to check LeClair for weapons. He removed a Luger from a shoulder holster, a sheath holding a stiletto, a KA-BAR strapped to his upper right arm, and two grenades. LeClair knew Cash would be suspicious if he didn't come fully armed, as usual.

LeClair gave the man a mischievous smile. "Don't let anything happen to those. I'll need them when I return."

The guard gave him a smug look in return, before ushering him inside. Along the way, LeClair let his eyes roam the perimeter, making a mental note of the guards' locations.

He was escorted through the entryway, past an oversized room that looked like it was used for entertaining, and then a few more steps to the right was Cash's office; a large A-frame contemporary room fully enclosed in glass to reveal a spectacular view of the mountains and a straight drop down to the water.

Cash smiled enigmatically from behind his large desk. "Ah good, you're here." He motioned toward his driver, Donghai, who stepped forward to frisk LeClair.

"Your hounds out front already took care of that," LeClair pointed out.

Cash gave him a dismissive glance, and nodded to Donghai to continue with the search.

LeClair shrugged. "And after all we've been through."

Cash smiled. "My private domain, you understand?"

LeClair nodded. "Sure, I understand. I wouldn't want the thought of me stabbing you in the back running around in your head."

Donghai motioned for LeClair to remove his jacket, and put his arms up in the air. Once he verified LeClair was unarmed, he nodded toward Cash then took his original position behind the desk.

LeClair slipped his jacket back on then took a seat opposite the desk. Cash held up a box of Cuban cigars.

LeClair selected one, then slid it under his nose to enjoy the aroma, then clipped it and lit it with a lighter.

"So, how was your trip to the states?" Cash inquired, as if he was feigning small talk.

LeClair took a hit off the Cigar then let it out, hesitating before answering. "Rather productive, I'd say."

Cash sat back in his leather chair, held the cigar between his fingertips and locked eyes on LeClair. "Am I to assume the problem has been taken care of?"

LeClair returned the stare. "I would say your problem with infiltrators no longer exists. Now, all that's needed is for you to complete our final transaction."

"I'm afraid there is a slight problem with that."

Sensing trouble, LeClair's body tensed, and he went on alert. He kept his eyes on the two men in front of him, while using his peripheral view to size up the room.

Cash opened the drawer under his desk and retrieved two photographs. "You see, something's been brought to my attention." He gave the photos a quick glance then handed them over to LeClair.

LeClair kept his expression firmly in check as he took a quick look at the photographs. The first photo was of him pulling Kyra from the explosion at the brownstone. The second was of him at the hospital watching over her.

224

"I imagine a beautiful woman like that could make you want to quit what you do, find a new arrangement and think about enjoying your life for a change?"

LeClair let his eyes linger on the photographs a little longer than he should, giving Cash the answer he needed. It was true; Kyra Ray was a woman that made him think of life in a different perspective, wondering if he should dare to hope for a better future. Was that something that was within his grasp? When he glanced back, Cash had a Glock 17 pointed toward his chest.

CHAPTER 46

LeClair's eyes turned cold. "So, I see you've been tracking me, again."

Cash flecked a piece of lint off his linen pants. "As I've told you many times, you don't get to be in my position by trusting the minions around you, Mr. LeClair. We've done this dance before, or have you forgotten how you received that scar?"

LeClair regained his calm demeanor. "Am I to assume this brings our fruitful relationship to a regrettable conclusion?"

"Even a highly skilled assassin such as yourself can be replaced. I should know. I paid to have you trained. I'll just have to train another."

Unfazed, LeClair stood up and let the photos drop to the floor. "How fortunate for me your employees don't like being referred to as minions..."

Cash had no time to react as Donghai snuck up behind him, wrapped a rope around his neck and pulled tight.

Cash's arms flailed in the air as he struggled to breathe, and the Glock dropped to the edge of the desk. He tried to slip his fingers underneath the rope. When he didn't succeed, he groped for Donghai who was just too strong.

226

LeClair walked over behind Cash then moved the computer monitor and keyboard so that it was directly in front of him as he continued to gasp for air.

LeClair typed in a few keys on the keyboard, bringing up the bank account information. "Now, to that little matter you failed to take care of," he said.

Cash remained defiant.

LeClair nodded toward Donghai, who pulled tighter on the rope making Cash gasp desperately for air. He resignedly typed in the required keys.

LeClair said, "The password please."

Donghai gave a good yank, until Cash's eyes began to bulge. He slowly nodded his head, knowing he was forced to comply. He typed the password onto the keyboard. The computer beeped.

Amount being transferred showed up on the computer screen.

LeClair put his hand up in the air, sending a signal to Donghai. "Not just yet.

When the term, *transaction complete* displayed, LeClair gave a quick nod to Donghai, who then released the rope from around Cash's neck.

Still struggling to breathe, he grabbed hold of his neck and sent a look of contempt toward LeClair. "Now you understand why I have cause to mistrust."

"It's the world you've created," LeClair said, feeling the taste of freedom within his grasp. His happiness was short-lived.

Within a few moments, Cash's arrogant, confidence returned. He proffered a sinister smile toward LeClair when The Chechen stormed into the room and thrust Kyra to the floor—her hands cuffed in front of her, and marks on her face. The backpack over her shoulder fell to the floor, and The Chechen now had his Beretta aimed toward LeClair.

Kyra struggled to get her bearings then picked herself up off the floor. When she did, she found herself staring into the eyes of LeClair—the man who killed her fellow agents; put a gun to her head, but chose not to shoot and then saved her life after the explosion.

Cash clapped his hands together. "That look is priceless. Oh, that's right; this is the first time the two of you have actually met. Interesting..."

Cash then swiveled around toward Donghai, and thrust a blade from his drawer right at his throat. "Now, we will have no further problems."

Stunned, Donghai grabbed at the blade to pull it out. A half a minute later, he fell face-forward to the floor.

Seizing the opportunity, LeClair sent a signal to Kyra with his eyes.

Simultaneously, she sent a swift kick to The Chechen, knocking the Beretta loose in his hand.

Then in one swift move, LeClair jumped for the Glock on the desk and filled with fury from years of nothing but bad memories; he planted a bullet in the center of Cash's chest.

Kyra followed up with a roundhouse kick to the side of The Chechen's head then came back around and kicked his legs out from under him. The Beretta dropped to the floor.

LeClair spun around and unloaded the Glock into The Chechen. "Thanks for the scars scumbag."

As The Chechen stumbled, Kyra dove across the floor and grabbed the Beretta. Rolling over on her back, she unloaded it into his chest as he barreled toward LeClair.

Riddled with bullets, he still surged forward. He was just about on top of LeClair, when he suddenly crashed to the floor with a loud thud.

LeClair stood in shock for a moment. "The guy was an ox!" He took a quick look at his watch, then immediately turned toward Kyra while she reached for her backpack.

"Shoot the glass!" he ordered.

Confused, Kyra looked at him as if he was mad. "What?"

"We've got thirty seconds to get the hell outta here!"

Kyra gave him another look, conflicted. "I'm not going anywhere with you."

LeClair aimed the Glock toward the glass. "Put aside what you think you know about me; just shoot out the goddamn glass!"

The man saved her life, twice, Kyra surmised as she slowly came around and complied. Simultaneously, they unloaded their weapons on the plate-glass window, until it shattered.

"What the hell's going on?" Kyra yelled.

"The place is wired; enough to blow the top of the mountain."

Before she had time to react, he pulled her toward the now shattered, plate-glass window then wrapped his arms tight around her, staring intently into her eyes.

"You're gonna have to trust me..."

As she nodded, they jumped through the shattered glass, somersaulted over the brush and sprang to their feet. LeClair aimed the Glock at the guard running toward them from the right. When he went down, LeClair pulled her toward the helicopter and ushered her inside. Seeing her eyes go wide, he turned back around and delivered a head shot to a second guard, and noticed others coming down off the roof.

He jumped inside the chopper and took his place in the pilot seat then prepared for takeoff. He opened the throttle, checked RPMs, gradually pulling up the collective, he pushed the pedal, and the chopper slowly lifted off the ground. As the earth below them started to rumble, he adjusted the cyclic and moved forward, the chopper shuddering as they eased off the mountain, and then out over the water.

Kyra turned around and watched the chateau slowly disappear from view, when suddenly, the top of the mountain erupted in a huge, thunderous explosion.

CHAPTER 47

LeClair's Yacht

Kyra slowly stirred awake, a quizzical look on her face, as if forgetting where she was. A quick look around reminded her that she was on LeClair's 65 foot Silverton Motor Yacht. She was alone in a queen bed in the guest room; her long, dark hair fanned out across the pillow and tanned legs tangled up in the crème satin sheets.

She pulled herself upright, allowing the events of the last twenty-four hours to visually run through her mind; the face-off with Colton Cash Tate and The Chechen then rushing to get away from an explosion. A quick reminder as to why she was here had her searching for her belongings. She signed with relief when she spotted her clothes and backpack on a leather chair across the room.

A light tap on the door brought her back to the present then a middle-aged woman dressed in a maid's uniform entered carrying a tray of food. Suddenly shy, Kyra pulled the sheets up to her neck to cover herself; which immediately had her wondering how she wound up naked in the first place.

"Where am I?" Kyra asked the maid, speaking in English.

The maid pretended not to hear. She set the tray down on the edge of the bed, and then politely exited the room.

"No speak'a'd English?" Kyra said once she was alone, again.

Her eyes darted around the room, realizing she was way out of her comfort zone. LeClair was somewhere on this boat; was she prepared to do what she needed to do? She had to for Brady.

She snatched a few strawberries and devoured them, and then jumped out of bed. First, she rifled through the contents in the backpack, smiling when she verified that nothing was damaged though the scuffle at the chateau. Then she slipped into the bathroom to take a quick shower, brush her teeth, and use the facilities. After less than twenty minutes, she stepped back into the guest room, and grabbed some fresh clothing. She slipped into a pair of shorts, a lace tank-top, and a pair of sandals, took one more look around the room, and slipped out into the passageway. Looking straight ahead was a small lounge area with the main suite on the opposite side; she assumed where LeClair slept.

She tiptoed up the set of the stars to the right that would take her to the upper level. There, she admired the main cabin with cherry wood cabinets, an oversized leather sofa and chairs, and a galley fully equipped with modern appliances and custom wood cabinets. The dinette area was raised and included the navigation center and entertaining features, including a wet bar and under-counter refrigerator. At the other end, a set of sliding glass doors opened to a teak wood deck, with a built-in sectional sofa.

She headed up another set of stairs off to the right leading to the upper deck, also set up for entertaining with a swim platform, and the cockpit.

And that's where she saw him.

Leaning against the railing with his arms folded across his chest in white shorts, a blue polo shirt, and a pair of deck shoes, LeClair looked like a freakin' model posing on the yacht for a world-wide travel magazine, and his masculinity was sexy as hell. Was he the same man who camouflaged himself in a Ghillie suit while scoping out his target, and then hid his face behind a ski mask while holding a gun point-blank to her head?

He penetrated her eyes with his, and his lips curved into a lazy smile. "You're not trying to sneak out on me now, are you?"

Kyra's breath caught in her throat, and her heart started to race in a way that she had never experienced before. She took a deep breath, and tried to get control of her thoughts. Could she be experiencing the physical chemical attraction that Tin and J.D. had discussed, claiming that was one of the triggers that kept LeClair from killing her?

Is lust—if that's really what it is—that powerful of a force that it can have that much of an impact between a man and a woman in their line of work?

Stammering, she said, "Actually, I was looking for you." She sure as hell wasn't going to admit that part of her was hoping to make a fast escape.

"Hmmm," LeClair said, amused as if he could see right through her.

"What time is it?" Kyra asked, stalling for time and trying to think of what to say.

"Nearly lunchtime," he said, as he strode toward her, closing the distance between them while keeping his eyes on hers until he was up close, trying to read her and see what she was thinking.

She really is breathtaking he thought to himself; a man could get lost in those eyes.

"It's that late?" Kyra said, stunned that she slept so long. But then again, she couldn't even remember going to bed.

"With all the excitement, you must have been exhausted. I was just heading into town, would you care to accompany me?"

He didn't wait for an answer; he merely placed his hand under her elbow and gently guided her back down the stairs, through the cabin, and out the sliding doors to the outer deck.

At the back ladder, he helped her down into a motorized inflatable boat. Once seated, he untied the rope, cranked the motor and they lapsed into a comfortable silence as he steered the boat inland toward the marina.

"Can I ask you something?" Kyra said after a few minutes.

"Anything."

"I woke up without any clothes on; did we--"

LeClair's head tilted back as he laughed out loud. "Did we have sex? Honey, if we did, you'd definitely remember."

***

The following morning, Kyra felt his strong fingers twirling her long hair and his warm lips brushing up against her cheek. She opened her eyes and stared into his, both of them satiated from an evening of powerful lust-filled romance, her face flushed and looking ravishing.

"Well hello," he said, fascinated by the depth of her Azure eyes. He traced a finger along her arm, sending a shiver down her spine.

"Hello yourself," she responded in a soft voice, filled with mixed emotions.

Their tanned and sweaty bodies were entwined beneath the sheets. Several vases filled with daisies sat around the room, an expensive bottle of wine, two half-filled glasses, and a plate of untouched fruits and vegetables sat on the settee.

He reached for a daisy, and traced it along her beautiful and exquisite body until she let out a whimper of pleasure.

"You like that, do you?"

"Hmm," she said, and another new experience stirred inside of her, emotions she had never been capable of feeling before. She tried to sit up, emotionally confused. How was it possible to feel such a powerful magnetism to one of the men responsible for the death of her fellow operatives?

LeClair playfully pulled her back down. "You're not trying to get away again now, are you?" He said as he let his lips dance over her forehead and then graze her cheek, and linger on her lips, letting his tongue tease and tantalize her.

When he looked into her eyes and held her gaze, it was as if the world stopped, and there was only the two of them. Right here, right now. Nothing else mattered. Then consumed with passion, he devoured her lips with his, and the lovemaking continued.

Several hours later, LeClair, replete after spending the day in bed with the most beautiful women he had ever met, lounged on the leather cushion of the upper deck enjoying a Cigar and a tall glass of iced tea. He wondered how long before his good fortune would end. She had confused feelings; he could see it in her eyes. He understood.

One minute, he was trying to kill her; the next he was saving her life. Hell, he was confused too, had been most of his life.

He let out a sigh and glanced down at a map on the table in front of him, and drew an outline.

Kyra came up the stairs from down below, dressed in a bright-colored bikini that showed off her every curve. Like a model on the catwalk, she sauntered toward him, and gave him a teasing smile.

Seeing the map in front of him, she looked him deadpan in the eye. "Lining up your next target?"

He frowned. "And we were having such a good time."

"I thought I'd go in the water; you feel like a swim?"

She could see he was overwhelmed with feelings; he came alive at the very sight of her.

"Hmm," he drawled. "I fear, you drenched in water, would only make me want you all over again, and there would be no swimming involved."

Kyra leaned down over him, allowing him to study her well-built physique. "You don't want me now?" She teased, while softly nibbling on his ear.

An animal sound escaped his throat. "Good God girl, what you have done to me."

Kyra draped her arms around his shoulders, and planted her lips on his, softly at first and then it deepened until it stirred the passion again.

He was instantly aroused. His hands devoured her every curve.

Then, Kyra pulled her lips away and smiled. "So," she said, mischievously. "That's why you saved my life, not once, but twice. It's my body you're after?" She traced a finger along his scar, as she gazed into his eyes – eyes that suddenly turned serious.

"I fear it's all of you I'm after," he said, boldly.

Kyra kissed him again, a long, passionate and memorable kiss. Then she forced herself away. Their fingertips touched as they drifted apart. She reached the edge of the boat, her eyes never leaving his.

"Killing doesn't bother you?"

He took a deep breath, trying to figure out the best way to respond. "You wouldn't have done the same? Tariq Jaffri and his men were arming terrorists."

"You killed three agents. Good men, with families."

A deep glimmer of regret appeared in his eyes. "I didn't know," he said with a voice that she barely heard. "I could never expect you to understand."

She studied him, torn. "You're right; you can't." Then she turned and dove into the deep blue sea.

***

LeClair let his mind wander to the unusual events that took place over the last few days, the last few years for that matter. He was a hired assassin, whether willingly, or not, that was what he was. Yet, here he was, hours later, after making love with a beautiful woman that he tried to kill, only a short time ago.

She was a target.

Longing for her to return, he glanced at his watch. He wanted to look into those exquisite eyes, rake his hands through her glorious hair and touch those luscious lips. Tell her he was a changed man.

As the time progressed, he knew.

He got up and walked around, looked out at the vast body of water, hoping she would just appear.

Worry furrowed his brow at the realization that she wasn't coming back. He reached under the dash for a set of binoculars and scanned the horizon.

Sensing it was bad enough, but reality hit him with a jolt of lightning when he caught sight of a small motor boat in the distance. Three people were on board, one of them a gorgeous specimen wearing a bright-colored bikini.

Moving as if his breath had been sucked out of him, he frantically searched the boat. He discovered Kyra's backpack, a carton of tampons inside.

His eyes looked pained as if he'd been pummeled in the gut.

Sitting behind the wheel of the 24 foot Sea Ray, J.D. cranked over the motor, while Tin pulled up anchor. Kyra towel-dried her hair, and kept her eyes glued to LeClair's boat.

"You sure of what you're doing?" Tin said to her, seeing how emotionally shattered she was.

When she turned her eyes to look at him they were as dark as night. "I followed orders. I did whatever was necessary to get close to him. It was a sanctioned kill."

Several moments later, the Silverton Yacht exploded. Fibreglass, parts, and cushions flew up into the air then came crashing back down with a huge splash.

Tin placed his arm around her as J.D. accelerated and the Sea Ray motored off away from the scene.

EPILOGUE

Operations Center, ATU

Kyra stood beside Barry West in front of several large CCTV Monitors showing satellite images of the cave in the Sherpur District.

On the screen, several Humvees rolled into the area then military personnel jumped out of the vehicles and surrounded the caves. Two members strategically placed an explosive device on the door to each cave, and then the signal given to take cover.

Seconds later, the doors burst open and soldiers entered with their weapons drawn then the caves thoroughly searched. Given the all clear, military personnel filed out, and jumped back into the Humvees.

As the Humvees left the scene, a Blackhawk Helicopter circled overhead then dropped a rocket down into the cave. Within seconds, Kyra watched the 3-D image mirage disappear from her sight.

"What about the families living on the hill above the cave?" Kyra asked; concerned about the Afghani family who saved her life.

West smiled. "As you requested; they're bulldozing the mud homes where your sniper was hiding out, and replacing them with homes with running water."

Kyra squeezed his hand. "Thank you."

241

He shook his head. "No thanks needed. They should never have been kicked out of their homes in the first place. Now, go on, Tin said you had him looking for something."

Kyra nodded then strode out of the communications room, down the sterile corridor, placed her hand on the biometric lock device, just to the right of the door. A green light appeared and the door slid open.

Kyra rejoined Tin and J.D. at their desks. J.D. had his feet up, relaxing with a wad of chew in his mouth.

Tin finished a can of espresso and crushed the can then his fingers resumed typing on the keyboard.

Kyra smiled. "What do you have for me?"

Tin glanced up at her, the smile he had a moment ago disappeared. "Money's gone. Accounts been completely wiped out."

Kyra plopped down into her own seat. "So does this mean what I think?"

J.D. glanced at Kyra. "What? What do you think?"

"He knew," she said, shaking her head. "He got away."

Confused, J.D. looked at Tin, and then back at Kyra. "Who got away? What are you two talking about?"

Kyra picked up the photos of LeClair; a surge of emotion went through her as she stared at the man. "Somehow, he slipped over the side of the boat, before the damn thing blew up. The man is invincible."

Tin looked deadpan at J.D. "LeClair ... he is alive."

Kyra leaned forward and glanced around the room, making sure that only Tin and J.D. heard what she was about to say. "There's something else that has been bothering me. When I went to talk to Hadley, he said to me, "Why can't you spies just leave me alone?" At the time, I thought he was just complaining because I was trying to get information. The more I thought about it, the more questions I had. Hadley was Brady's asset, and he was all about making money. As long as he kept giving info, he kept getting paid."

J.D. shrugged. "So he did a double-cross and got paid extra? What don't you understand?"

"I don't understand why he would do that. The U.S. was a steady supply for him. He helped with information on a few occasions, received payment, and kept coming back. He bought that apartment building, because he thought he had a steady supply. He told Brady about the arms deal in the first place. So why risk losing his steady paycheck, and tell Cash that two agents were in the area. We sure as hell didn't give Hadley the heads up that we were coming; we were tracking him for crying out loud."

Tin was shaking his head up and down. "Yeah, I see what you're getting at. Hadley didn't rat you out."

The three of them looked at each other at the same time that the realization hit them square in the face.

"We have a mole."

***

Kyra walked toward the memorial where they buried her parents, and hundreds of others from the

243

Pentagon and Flight 77. When she was about ten feet away, she stopped in her tracks: someone placed dozens and dozens of daisies all around.

Kyra spun around and let her eyes scan the area. "LeClair," she whispered to herself.

Thank you so much for purchasing and reading Sanctioned Kill. I appreciate it more than you know. Readers and word of mouth are crucial to an author's success. If you read the book and enjoyed it, I would be honored if you would consider leaving a one or two line review at Amazon.

Thank you so much.

Website: http://writercrhiatt.com/
Twitter: https://twitter.com/McSwainandBeck
Blog: http://mcswainandbeck.com/
Facebook: https://www.facebook.com/CRHIATT
Feel free to email me for updates, or information on upcoming books at AuthorCRHIATT@gmail.com